Winter Symphony on Lake Mattamuskeet

A Love Story

by

Georgia Denton Warren

ISBN: 0615806120

ISBN-13: 9780615806129

Acknowledgements

Through God all things are possible.

Friends of Mattamuskeet Lodge: Locals from the area who tirelessly contributed their time and effort towards the restoration of Mattamuskeet Lodge.

I want to thank Jordan Taylor for being my wordsmith and editing the manuscript for clarity and coherence of thought. I would like to congratulate Jordan on her 2013 graduation from N. C. State University, earning a degree of Bachelor of Arts in English with a concentration in Creative Writing.

To the most talented artist I know, Stacey Warren Porter, whose artistic creativity and design of the book cover captured the true essence of this love story.

Loving thanks to my wonderful children: Stacey Warren Porter (mother of my granddaughter Quinn), Ana and Kenan Warren, and to my son-in-law Brian Porter (husband to Stacey and dad to Quinn). Thank you so much for your unconditional love and support.

To my wonderful family, whose lively lives make life fun.

I express a heartfelt thanks to Madelyn Lockhart.

I'm deeply grateful to Steve Lockhart for taking me on the road trip to Lake Mattamuskeet that started it all, and for the many months afterwards patiently pushing me to finish something I started.

This book is a testament to how a person's imagination can make an abandoned building come to life.
Georgia Denton Warren
Imagination is more important than knowledge....
Albert Einstein

Chapter 1

Margaret lay still beneath the layered covers. The early morning ice crystals etching the window made her pull the warmth closer to her chin, wiggling her sock feet. Margaret basked in the comfortable position, gazing out beyond the frosted window towards the sky, and thinking how today marked the day of their return. Staring quietly from beneath the overstuffed quilts, something in the distance caught her attention, making her smile. The low humming from beyond the forest told her that they had begun arriving. The blend of sounds of the returning waterfowl calmed her mind, inspiring her to pray for their safety while they visited the area, but as her thoughts wandered further her smile turned sad, knowing her prayers had not been answered for the return of the person she had met during one of the birds' visits, a person she had not seen in decades. Every day since he had left she longed to see him again.

The early morning stillness heightened the distant sound, awakening her deep-seated memories. The constant sound slowly encouraged them to take root and grow, shaping into a visually recognizable image that tugged at her emotions: the outline of his face, his deep blue eyes staring at her with a look of desire, soothing her emotions and relaxing her thoughts, making it hard for her to turn away. His kiss besieged her drowsy heart, making her want more from him, only to see his face quickly fading away and leaving her once again.

The honking sound outside the window broke her trance. Looking out into the dawn light, the geese caught her attention. Every bird, like fighter pilots in V formation, flew slightly above the bird in front of him, flapping their wings in the direction of Lake Mattamuskeet.

The tears welled up in her eyes. Rolling onto her side, she tightly squeezed her pillow and hoped for a repeat of the memory. The tears streaming down her cheeks made Margaret long for the familiar sound that once connected her to him all those years ago. She felt paralyzed as she listened to the prolonged sound carrying through the dense copse of undergrowth that lay beneath the thick woodlands beyond the house. The sound grew louder as the sun rose. The bright light coming up over the horizon warmed everything in its path. The reflection of light hitting the water made the birds' pitch higher, each note reverberating against the thin plate of window glass that kept the loud sound from totally entering the bedroom.

Their ambient sound persuaded Margaret to quickly get up. The evocative message was letting her know that they had arrived, and the echoing helped to stimulate her steps to hurry to their location, but a different sound from across the hall made her waver. The rumbling she had not heard in weeks made her feel energized enough to rush to get dressed.

The sun caught a glimpse of her as she looked out of the window. The carpet of frost told her it was going to be a cold day. The glistening view made it clear enough to see across the field separating the Windley farm from the Rogers'. Paul Rogers, like her dad, Thomas, had inherited his farm from his family.

Seven years ago Lillian Rogers had lost Paul to a fatal heart attack. Now both women felt the same loss after Margaret's dad Thomas died in his sleep at the age of seventy-eight, saddening Margaret far more than she could cope with at times. The funeral had been emotionally painful; Margaret had cried softly into a handkerchief throughout the whole thing, not wanting to say good-bye to the man who had given her true meaning in life when at times nothing she did made sense. Regardless of the choices Margaret had made, Thomas had cherished everything about his daughter; their father daughter bond was indissoluble.

The distressing months to follow had gradually dissolved as she was smothered unconditionally by her loving son John and the many in the community who had constantly stopped in to visit. Throughout those months, her painting had helped give her the emotional stability to adjust. The heartening aspect of Thomas's death was that it had come after the farming season and at the beginning of the bird migratory season, a transition that helped her to move on from her grief and to appreciate the years she'd had with her father.

With John in college, the farm was a bit much for Margaret to manage alone. Now Margaret and Lillian turned to Steve Jessup and his sons, Jacob and Henry, to farm the land. The Jessups own the land on the northern side of Lake Mattamuskeet. Steve and Melissa Jessup's sons Jacob and Henry lived close to their parents. The oldest Jacob was married with two children, but Henry, who was the same age as Margaret, was single. They both had grown up together, and had even dated a few times, occasionally, just to enjoy each other's company.

As Margaret finished putting on her bedroom slippers, there was a faint knock at the door.

"Hey Mom, are you up?"

Margaret quickly jumped off the bed to open the door. She beamed with joy as she stared at John, touching his face, combing back his hair with her hands. "Good morning, son" she said. "Did you sleep well?"

His piercing blue eyes lit up as he smiled at her, bending his 6'2" stature to give her a hug. His embrace made her feel less lonely in this big old farmhouse. John had been attending State College in Raleigh, and was home for the holidays. It was a good feeling having him around spending time with her. Margaret very rarely traveled to Raleigh to see John. She wanted to know he was safe, and so had given him the family's newer truck, while she had kept the older one for herself, making the long drive to Raleigh more difficult. And Margaret's responsibilities kept her close to home; the furthest she usually went was when she and Lillian managed the trip to Greenville to pick up supplies they could not find at Gibbs Store.

As Margaret headed down to the kitchen, the temperature fell slightly below 45 degrees. The oil heater in the living room helped raise the temperature upstairs, but it couldn't handle heating the whole house, leaving some rooms colder. Walking into the cold kitchen had John quickly opening the door to the old wood stove and stirring the smoldering coals. As he strode out of the door for firewood, Margaret reminded him to get his coat. The cold air brought a chill through her body, making Margaret reach up to grab a sweater off the hook on the wall. As John threw in the firewood he talked excitedly about finishing up his senior year at State and going off to law school. As he talked, he stoked the fire with the poker, its hot ashes flying around the room and dying out before hitting the floor.

"Hey Mom, what time is the mail coming?"

Margaret smiled at him. "John, you haven't been away that long! The same time as always, unless Ms. Harriet keeps Jim longer than usual. Hopefully, he should be here with the mail about 9:30 a.m." Everyone knew Ms. Harriet interrogated Jim whenever he delivered her mail. She had to catch up on the community gossip.

Margaret grabbed her easel, paint, brushes and canvas and piled them beside the front door. John finally had a fire going in the kitchen's wood stove, making the room warmer. As he threw in another log, he watched his mom fill a jug with water. John knew this time of year gave his mother hope.

Smiling, he said, "You headed down to the water's edge? I heard them calling you this morning." John knew his mother's passion for painting was something that had begun long before he was born, and that this time of year, nothing could keep her away from the brushes and canvas.

Margaret sighed as she turned off the water. "The recent rains have kept me from driving down to the big oak tree. I can only maneuver part of the way; then, I have to lug everything to the landing. I'd hoped it would warm up some, but I can't wait much longer."

John stirred the boiling grits to keep the coarsely ground corn from sticking and forming lumps while his mother got her things together. As she came into the kitchen, she reached up on the shelf for the iron skillet to fry the eggs in. Reaching in the crock container, she scooped a tablespoon of pig fat into the pan. She stared down, watching the heat melt the thick creamy lard into clear crackling oil. Cracking the cold slimy eggs into the pan made the hot grease spit at her, quickly consuming the raw egg and frying the clear edges to a crisp brown.

John watched his mom take the spatula to flip the eggs, trying not to break the yolks. Margaret knew John liked his yolk runny. John slowly stirred the burbling grits. Concerned, he lay the spoon beside the thickened mixture and turned to stare at his mom.

"Mom, I can go ahead and carry your things for you."

Margaret stood gazing into his caring blue eyes, seeing a part of someone she had not seen in years. As he grew older, his looks and mannerisms were more like his father's. The similarity brought tears to her eyes. Grabbing the spoon, she quickly looked away to spoon the mixture onto a plate.

"No son, I've got it. Now you eat your breakfast and get on out of here, or you'll be late picking up Claire."

John salt and peppered his eggs, blending them into his grits. Taking a spoon, he devoured the yellow mixture. He glanced at the clock. He didn't have much time. It was nearly 9:15 a.m., and he had told Claire he would pick her up at 9:30. After grabbing his coat, he reached down to give his mom a hug and kiss on the cheek.

As he stuffed his coat pockets with biscuits wrapped in a napkin, he said, "Claire and I are going to Greenville to do some Christmas shopping. I'm sure I'll get hungry watching her shop. I might even sneak over to the jewelry store." This sudden bit of information made Margaret quickly pull her hands out of the hot dish water, drying them on her apron as she turned, smiling affirmatively at John. Putting her warm hands on his shoulder, she said, "I've got some cash saved up John. I know you two are ready to live your lives together after graduating from college."

John stood to give his mom a hug. "Thanks for your generosity, but I'm just looking."

They both laughed, clinging tightly to each other. Margaret gave John a kiss on the cheek before he put on his coat. After zipping it up and reaching for the doorknob, he looked back at his mother and said, "We should be back around 4:00 p.m. I'll be on time to carry Lillian her supper; if that's okay with you, Mom. I'll take mine over there too; I know she must be feeling lonely since Paul's death."

Pleased, Margaret smiled affirmatively at John; she loved his empathetic ways. He got that from his grandfather, always caring about everyone else first. Margaret opened the refrigerator, "I've got supper done, John. All I'll need to do is warm up the pot roast."

As she shut the refrigerator door, a red circle on the calendar caught her eye. Suddenly she realized Christmas would be here in 2 weeks, and as always John had tagged a spruce tree over the summer to cut down. Margaret had already planned a party for Saturday week to decorate the tree. The usual family and friends came every year. Lillian and Louise, Claire and her family, and the Jessups all helped to put together the annual event since Thomas's death.

With her dad's death and John being in college, Henry Jessup came around more and more often to help with the daily chores. Margaret secretly thought he was hanging around for her home cooking, hoping Margaret wouldn't ask him to leave.

Occasionally he spent the night, but most nights she wanted to be alone. Every Christmas Margaret held her breath, hoping Henry would not propose to her. Lillian urged Margaret to give Henry a chance, telling her that Henry was probably getting tired of being the only one who seemed to care about keeping their relationship going. But everyone knew how crazy Henry was about Margaret; he would wait a lifetime for her.

Chapter 2

It was almost mid December. Margaret stood on the porch waving goodbye to John, holding a cup of strong coffee, already anxious as the faint sound of the waterfowl could be heard coming from the distance. She gazed out at the glistening front yard; the mud holes from the recent rain, the barb wire fence, and the sodden brown field beyond that was stabbed with dried corn stalks stripped from the recent harvest. It was a decent drive from the house to the road; Thomas had built the farmhouse far away from the road but close to the edges of the woods.

The two story house, wood, painted white, had a raised foundation and a deep railed front porch that stretched all the way across the front of the house. It was lined with rocking chairs filled with cushions comfortable enough to sit for hours, where most evenings from early spring to late fall she and her dad had sat rocking to the chirping of the crickets and talking about their days, or listening to Thomas tell John stories about the early days. Lingering for a moment, Margaret's fingers outlined the arm rest of the rocker.

Walking behind the house, she unlatched the barn doors. An old green Chevrolet truck rested inside. Its sturdy stake racks made of seasoned wood helped to contain higher loads, like when she hauled feed to the cows. In the cab, the cracked worn seat was covered with a stretched green nylon seat cover. Through it, the rough grooves in the worn plastic could still be felt. The truck, like everything else in the barn, had been her father's.

Margaret set her coffee on the seat and then backed out of the barn. With her left foot she pushed down the clutch, then put the gear in first. Not wanting to spill her coffee, Margaret gently eased off the clutch. The clouds shouldered over the tall trees, left sparse from the fall season. Margaret stopped at the chicken coop, dragging out the plastic jug filled with feed and corn she'd ladled from the sack in the tack room. The pen, built by her father, ran twenty-five feet out from the length of the left side of the barn and adjoined a room inside that had been converted into a roost. Margaret liked feeding the hens, who lived their lives in the same tiny patch, not caring whether today it was dirt or mud. She'd tried letting a couple run free, hoping they'd stay close, but the first hen wandered away and was never seen again. The next had probably become a quick victim of some hungry stray dog, who had left only feathers to identify that the hen had ever existed.

Unlatching the coop's wire door, she entered its odor of droppings. She shut the door behind her, turning with her arms stretched out as she raised the plastic jug. She flung the feed and watched for a moment as the hens pecked it up with their stiff jerks, clucking, scratching, and bobbing their heads among the speckled droppings and wet feathers. Turning the spigot, she filled their metal tray with water. In the barn, the chickens were making their noises under the heat lamp. Margaret walked toward the boxes, shooing the setting hens and watching them run through the hole and down the ramp into the enclosed coop with the others.

Margaret reached in the boxes to collect the brown eggs, carefully putting the warm eggs in her coat pockets.

She eased herself back into the truck and turned the wheel to slowly begin circling back along the barb wire, following the fencing towards the front of the house. At the front steps she shifted into reverse and backed up, getting out and unlatching the tailgate. Back inside the house, she put the fresh eggs in the wire basket hanging from the ceiling.

Margaret walked out to the porch and picked up her cup from earlier, taking a couple of sips of cold coffee before tossing the rest into the yard. She began to load her art supplies meticulously into the truck's wooden bed. After putting the canvas and paints in the cab of the truck, she turned to walk back up the steps. The sound of an engine roaring caused her to pause. She could see the mailman driving down towards the house, which Jim did when he had a package or certified mail; she knew her catalog orders should be arriving soon, but this was a little too soon.

The Buick bounced up and down whenever it hit a hole, Jim's head playing to the rhythm and then slowing as the old Buick station wagon pulled to a stop beside the truck. Jim lowered his baritone voice to a more emphatic tone to ask Margaret how she and John were doing. Before Margaret could answer, Jim continued talking, apologizing for being late. Ms. Harriett had kept him longer than usual; she'd wanted to know about the new family that moved into the Johnson's place.

Margaret laughed. "I'm not surprised. If I need to know the local happenings, I'll just call Ms. Harriett." Jim laughed along with her.

Peering into the Buick, Margaret didn't see any packages. She watched as Jim reached for the stack of mail seated on the passenger seat. He fumbled with an envelope before giving her a pen and a pad to sign. A troubled expression crossed the fine lines of Margaret's face as she looked down at the letter. Her face grew pale.

Margaret tried to control the trembling of her voice as she asked: "Jim, where do I sign?"

She gripped the pen tightly in her hand as she looked down at the letter. There was something mistaken about the name - she didn't recognize the first name but knew the last. Before she could finish signing her name her hand began to shake.

Noticing this, Jim wanted to reach for Margaret's hand but hesitated. Instead, in a subtle voice he asked, "Ms. Margaret, are you alright? You look a little pale."

Margaret had been listening to him, but at the back of her mind a memory was taking shape, blurring the sound of his voice. She paused uneasily, suddenly feeling her face flush with embarrassment. Realizing this, Margaret began to laugh. "I'm fine. I've been busy carrying supplies to the truck; my grip is a little tired."

Quietly she looked down, still shocked as she looked at the return name on the envelope: "William Ashton, New York, New York". Margaret was searching her memory for the name, trying to understand the relationship to the only Ashton she ever knew.

Jim took the pen and pad back from her, smiling, his voice getting a little softer. "We don't deliver many letters all the way from New York since the Lodge shut down. Matter of fact, Lawrence Davenport got at least two or three a month, but ever since Lawrence unexpectedly died of a heart attack I don't think I've delivered a single one."

Margaret smiled back. She knew Jim liked to gossip more than Ms. Harriett. She laughed, attempting to play it off. "Oh, just someone I sold a painting to several years ago," she replied. "I guess it's time for another."

Jim stared at Margaret as though he waited for the rest of the story, but tipped his hat at her when he realized he wasn't going to get it, saying, "Well have a good day, Ms. Margaret."

Margaret stared back at him. "Jim, I'll see you at church on Sunday." Margaret actually liked listening to Jim's baritone voice as he sang in the church choir.

Margaret could feel her heart racing as she walked away, sliding her fingernail under the flap and hesitating before opening the letter. She slipped the thin paper from the envelope, and took in a deep breath and slowly exhaled. She reached inside her coat pocket for her reading glasses. Putting them on hanging almost to the edge of her nose, she nervously adjusted them to eye level.

"Dear Ms. Margaret Windley,
If you are reading this, it must have made it to you. My name is William Ashton. You do not know me, but you knew my brother, John Ashton; apparently you both met during his stay at a hunting lodge in Lake Mattamuskeet. Recently our father Howard Ashton passed away, leaving me in charge of his estate. I have found information in some of my father's things I need to discuss with you. Enclosed is my business card, giving you my address and phone number. My family and I will be traveling to the Outer Banks to visit with friends on Sunday, December 20, and I would like to meet with you that afternoon. Please give me a call to schedule a time that would be convenient for us to meet.
Best Regards,
William Garrett Ashton"

Margaret stood frozen, her mouth slightly open, lips shaping each word as she read quietly. She took a deep shuddering breath. "Why does he need to meet with me?" she whispered to herself. She replayed all the words in the letter, hoping to find the answer. Baffled, she stared off into the distance, not focusing on anything in particular, and for a moment she was taken aback. Feeling her legs weaken, she slowly sat down in the chair at the kitchen table, trying to understand what it all meant.

Margaret finally put down the letter and got up without thinking. She walked over to the sink and absently turned on the cold water tap to rinse the dry mud off her boots. She felt drawn back to the letter, stunned by this unexpected revelation. Once again she tried to make sense of the words.

Feeling like she would suffocate in the small room, Margaret turned to walk over to the kitchen chair. The seat felt warm from her recent stay. Lifting up her foot, she slid on one boot and then the other. She paused, the written words disturbing her thoughts. A sudden twinge of pain pierced through her heart. Catching her breath, she felt a yearning for a period in her life that was too painful to relive. She forced the thought away, shaking her head as she picked through the other mail, smiling as she reached for the large envelope addressed from "The University of North Carolina School of Law," to "John Ashton Windley".

Her thoughts soon returned to the kitchen table, where the open letter piqued her curiosity. She gave in, taking the business card and calling the number listed. Margaret listened to the ringing. She took in her breath slightly but continued to hold the phone to her ear. She wanted to hang up when the answering machine came on, but instead she left a short message including her phone number. The anguish of the past had managed to slowly crystallize itself throughout the years, but within an hour her thoughts of that time in her life had flourished, making Margaret wonder how the past had caught back up with her so quickly.

Margaret put the business card aside. She needed to get out, get some fresh air. She hurriedly packed a lunch and jumped in the driver's seat, putting the basket on the front seat. She took in a deep breath. For the first time in years since John Ashton left she felt there was a possibility her son John would get information about his father. Knowing this left Margaret feeling hopeful, hopeful that she may also find out why he had never returned to Lake Mattamuskeet, to her. Stepping inside the front door, she grabbed another basket with food, a small chest, and a change of clothes which she placed on the floorboard. She pulled the door shut and went through a mental checklist. She knew it would be hard for her to turn back once she got down the rugged path.

Sitting behind the wheel, she rubbed her palm on the smooth steering wheel of the 1959 Chevrolet truck. It had been kept in good shape by her father, who was the first to store it in the old barn. Margaret was not so caring at times, she sometimes liked to keep the truck parked under the oak tree as close to the house as she could get it. Then when she was missing her father, Margaret only had to look out of the window. Even four years later, the memory of her father was still fresh in her mind. Sometimes on certain times of the day when the light was just right, she could almost see him sitting behind the wheel, wearing his favorite worn cap advertising Farmall tractors.

Chapter 3

December 12, 1981 was 42 degrees with the sun shining, warming the earth enough to liquefy the frost to a glistening dew. Margaret's faded Levi jeans were worn into a comfortable fit and covered the tops of her leather boots; a wool jacket covered a shirt and a cardigan sweater hand knitted by Lillian Rogers. Without looking into the rearview mirror she tied her long unruly hair into a ponytail. Although just turning forty, Margaret still received many compliments on her good looks. Most said she was a spitting image of her mom, whose family came from a prominent Ohio family which had settled in New Holland, a small town established during the early 1900's and located along the southern shoreline of Lake Mattamuskeet. She looked at her watch: ten-twenty. She had called Lillian over an hour ago to tell her she was on her way. The days' events seem to be stalling her every effort, slowing her journey.

Turning the key, she listened as the warm engine roared. She shifted into first and headed out. Frost lightly crusted the edges of the windshield, but the sun's warmth soon thawed out the glass. Her thoughts were filled with words written by a person she'd never met, but who wanted to meet her, constantly asking herself the same question, "What information did William Ashton have for her?" Margaret felt a ripple of fear trek up her spine as she drove.

At the end of the long driveway she slowed, downshifting as she pulled onto the paved road. She drove only a few feet before making a hard right off the hardly traveled road and stopping at a mailbox beautified by a painting of a Tundra Swan. She grabbed the mail from inside the box and shut its door, whispering to herself that she needed to touch up the fading swan. It was Lillian who had taught Margaret how to paint, when she was eight, after her mother's tragic death. Lillian and Paul Rogers had been married for 43 years when Paul died of a massive heart attack. The two had married when Lillian was twenty-two years old. Paul was the only love of her life.

Now Lillian was in poor health from a recent bout of pneumonia, which had caused her to be bedridden since Thanksgiving. Driving up to the house, Margaret thought about the letter as she stared ahead at the landscape with its winter grass, watching the sheep feeding in silence. The soft sunlight made everything feel serene.

Margaret grabbed the basket from the floorboard and stepped up onto the porch. Opening the screen door, she knocked on the back door, hollering to let Lillian know she would let herself inside. She held the screen door with her left foot as she found the key to turn the lock. She unloaded the basket on the counter, filling the tray with a multitude of morning goodies. She walked towards the front of the house to the bedroom. Lillian, still in her bathrobe and pajamas, sat in a chair beside the bed, smiling despite her ill health. Placing the tray on the table beside the bed, Margaret apologized for her lateness as she hugged Lillian.

"How are you feeling? You look better than yesterday; has Doc stopped in to see you?"

Lillian held Margaret's hand as she spoke, "Doc just left. He gave me another shot to ward off pneumonia. I do feel better. You don't know how much I appreciate this; I don't know what I would do without you Margaret." Tears welled up as she continued talking. Lowering her voice, Lillian whispered that she knew how painful this time of year was for Margaret, but when they called, it was their sound she hoped helped to sooth the pain.

"I heard them calling you this morning, letting you know they had arrived," she softly whispered as she held on to Margaret's hand. "If Doc hadn't forbid me to get out, I would be sitting in that ole pickup truck beside you, headed towards their calling."

Margaret lightly squeezed Lillian's hand. "I know, I know, but right now we need to keep you indoors until you get better." Not wanting to mention the letter, Margaret stood up to fill the water pitcher beside the bed.

Lillian stared at Margaret inquisitively, saying, "Margaret is something wrong?"

Margaret put the pitcher down, smiling. Not wanting to worry Lillian, she calmly said, "Lillian, I'm fine. I'm just anxious to get down to the water to see the waterfowl. I'm hoping they all migrated back this year. I guess I'm being a little selfish, but I hope none of them were killed, and I still hope they all returned back to the Lake."

With tears streaming down her face, Lillian hugged Margaret, saying, "I know, dear. I feel the same."

Before leaving Margaret promised to send John over with dinner. Lillian had babysat John as a baby while Margaret helped her dad tend to the farming; Lillian and John had a special relationship. It was a shame that Lillian could not have any children; she would have made a wonderful mom.

Margaret repeated the same words she did every visit before leaving. "Lil, why don't you come stay with John and I at the house? I've got enough room for us all."

Looking at Lillian, she knew this was her home, that her response would be the same that it always was: "You know why Margaret, everything we love is in our homes, our memories. My reason is Paul and yours is Thomas."

The sound of a car pulling up to the house cut off the old argument - Lillian's sister Louise had come to stay with her. Margaret knew Louise, a retired nurse, would take good care of Lillian. Louise normally left at 3:00 to care for her husband who stayed at a nursing home; since they were short-handed at night Louise worried about the care he was getting, and would feed and bathe him before heading home.

Louise was sixty-seven and a bit taller than Lillian, with short gray hair. Both were very close and devoted to each other. Louise had worked, up until 6 years ago, at a hospital in Greenville. When her already ailing husband had a massive stroke, Louise retired to care for him until she was physically no longer able. Since Lillian had become ill, Louise drove the eight miles every day to care for her sister. Neither could have children. They had never known why until a doctor at the hospital where Louise worked performed a simple test that revealed a blockage preventing the successful passage of the fertilized egg to the uterus. The doctor told Louise that surgery could be used to correct the problem, but by then Louise was already 47 years old. With an already ailing husband, she knew it was not feasible for her to have a child now. Lillian's curiosity led her to call for an appointment with the same doctor, but then the week before the appointment she realized that regardless of the outcome, at 51 it was too late. The yearning of motherhood subsided when Margaret gave birth to John.

Anxious to get going, Margaret let Lillian know John would bring supper at 6:00. Hugging Lillian and Louise good-bye, Margaret grabbed the empty basket before walking out the door.

Turning into the sun, Margaret began the short journey to her destination. Staring ahead, she noticed the Ford truck on the other side of the road slowing down as though about to stop. Not having time to waste, Margaret never slowed down and instead threw up her hand to acknowledge Henry. She hated to do that to Henry, but she had no more time to waste.

Margaret turned the truck off the highway onto an unpaved road, a faint cloud of dirt floated slowly in the still air. Driving down the dirt road, her thoughts took her further down, slowing to analyze the massive structure whose windows were boarded up, its doors padlocked, left vacant after years of providing housing to many who came to the area to hunt. Now most hunters stayed with area locals or purchased homes exclusively for the seasonal hunting.

Mattamuskeet Lodge located in Hyde County once had a reputation as one of the favorite hunting lodges in the country. During its heyday, guests migrating to the North Carolina lake had included governors, senators, congressmen, state representatives, lawyers, doctors and other members of the wealthy. Even under duress, the Lodge was an unforgettable presence. Its 112-foot observation tower for viewing the lake, topped with a flying goose weather vane, resembled a lighthouse, and the Lodge, a grand manor. The central three-story section was flanked by smaller wings on either side, and the building was set against a backdrop of lush greenery. The quiet canal waters of Lake Mattamuskeet that formed the Lodge's front lawn and back yard mirrored the imposing structure.

The truck hesitated for a second as Margaret locked her eyes on a hunter walking ahead carrying a shotgun. He reminded her of someone she once knew; the fading memory of him quickly appeared, then left. Inwardly, Margaret suffered the quiet trepidation of a woman who felt a strong connection to the building that stood abandoned, filled with memories boarded up inside that had forever changed her life. As she stared at the highest point of the building, a sudden flash reflected off the copper and awoke memories better left undisturbed. The dark moment rumbled through her soul, touching scars left by memories too beautiful to be forgotten, but painful enough to suffocate in. She pushed them back inside, leaving only an intermittent blur fading through her mind.

Margaret closed the opening of her jacket, a sharp chill making her reach for the truck's heater. A block of winter sun splayed across the windshield as she turned her mind around to reality. After driving down further, she slowed, staring off to her right at a fading, barely visible "no trespassing" sign held up with only one nail. Margaret got out to hammer the nail further into the tree, hoping it would deter any would-be hunters. The land, once owned by an attorney in Richmond, had been purchased twenty years back by an unknown. It was overgrown and apparently forgotten. Some said an anonymous wealthy family from up North had purchased the property for hunting; if so, it was apparent they had lost all interest in the property. The land was located beside her own property, but was the best of all that around the lake; it had a deep cove cut far up into the land, giving many birds a safe place to migrate and hatch their young. Occasionally, Margaret would trespass with her pad and pencil to sketch some of the many rare waterfowl that frequented the small recess in the shoreline of the property.

Margaret drove a short distance before turning down the narrow dirt road. Shifting the gears, she turned, following the ruts in the worn path. Her tires slid on the mud and she slowed, fishtailing. She let the steering wheel guide itself until the road curved as the truck approached a bend in the woods. Slowly braking, Margaret stopped in front of a gate with a posted sign: "No Hunting". Margaret searched in the truck for the key to let herself in the gate. She drove through, parking on the other side and then closing and locking the gate behind her. Back in the truck, she cranked down her window, taking in a deep breath of cold crisp air. The smell charged her nostrils. She took in another and for a second closed her eyes, quickly opening them as she bumped and slid along the grooves filled with sodden leaves and twigs. Only a few leaves remained on the otherwise bare limbs. Looking through the trees, Margaret caught glimpses of the lake. This was as far as the truck could go.

Margaret cut the truck's engine off, coasting a little closer before getting out and walking the rest of the way. As she slid out of the driver's seat, the noise of the birds could immediately be heard, energizing Margaret as she grabbed her art supplies. For a moment she closed her eyes as she listened to their beautiful sound, each feathery bird playing their own instrument, orchestrating a beautiful winter symphony.

This land was privately owned, left to her by a father who knew the twenty acres was priceless. The area gave Margaret endless inspiration to paint moments filled with the most exotic birds ever seen in the area. She had received many offers for the "Hunter's Paradise," but declined until now; John's acceptance to law school was going to be costly, and so after the first of the year she would meet Dan Miller at the bank and sign the papers to sell him the twenty acres. She would be there as soon as the bank opened, hoping to keep all this from John. She knew John would not approve of the sale, but the money Dan offered would be more than enough to pay his way through law school. Though saddened by this, Margaret knew it was financially the best thing for John to continue his education.

Reaching for the bucket on the ground, she put all she knew it would hold inside and then climbed the wooden steps her father had built to allow her to safely get to the wooden landing. Two of the boards had recently been replaced by Henry, who worried when he saw that the wooden platform was no longer as secure as it had been when it was built by her dad over twenty years before. Henry also had replaced the rope, which was frail from years of rubbing on the branch, and put in a pulley system, making it easier for Margaret to pull up the load.

The creaking sound of stepping onto the platform reminded Margaret of the worn barn floor. Standing on the covered landing, her eyes caught the most magnificent view imaginable. Every year she was awed by the beauty of this land. Mattamuskeet Lake was framed by woodlands and fringed marshes, the lake's glimmering expanse made it a water magnet for migratory birds and unfortunately a mecca for hunters. In winter, flocks of snow geese and tundra swans turned the water white in places. Their presence and the sound of their song was what kept Margaret believing in a higher being, giving her hope that she would soon find out the truth about the person who had once come into her life, changing it forever.

Looking out at the miraculous sight made her want to get closer. After stepping down from the platform, she quietly picked her way to the water's edge. The wet leaves sparkled like mirrors, reflecting a distorted image of herself in the blackberry water, which was stirred by the birds' movement as their own reflections passed over the water's surface.

Margaret stared out across the water. Closing her eyes, she inhaled, taking in a deep breath and holding the moment. A light breeze touched her cheek, chilling her thoughts. Margaret knew this isolated area of the lake gave the migratory birds refuge from the hunters who killed these magnificent creatures as a sport; most had the birds stuffed to hang in their plush offices or country homes. Knowing that inevitably many of them would be harmed brought tears to her eyes. Wiping them, she hurried back to finish unloading the big wash bucket, then lowered it. She climbed the sturdy steps back down, quickly walking to the truck for the final load. Her brow beaded with perspiration as she carried the last load towards the landing. She stood for a moment, her mouth gaped open trying to catch her breath. The day had gotten off to a peculiar start, making her rush herself before the light of the day changed everything around her. A hunting dog could be heard yowling in the distance, and the sound of a shotgun drifting through the still air disturbed her thoughts.

Reaching in her pocket, Margaret unfolded the worn picture and took a moment to stare at the couple beautifully dressed in their formal wear, with their bright smiles, trying to hold tightly to each other. If she would have known the inevitable, Margaret would have never let go of him. The picture was dated December 22, 1962. Other than her memories this was the last visual image of him she had left. Written on the back was the last known evidence of how he felt about her, "My Dearest Margaret, You have stolen my heart. Love, John." That night Nathanial had photographed this picture, capturing the special moment. Margaret had been grateful when Lawrence delivered the valuable photograph after it was sent to the Lodge with no return address.

Knowing she was being foolish, Margaret traced the contours of his face with her finger. Every year on this date she went back to the place they first met and took a moment to reminisce on her memories, yearning to see him again. Margaret stared at the photograph. She remembered the sound of his voice that night, softly whispering to her how special she was to him. As she stood isolated from any human life, the words resonated through her mind over and over again. Now, after all these years, Margaret was finally going to find out the truth.

This sudden revelation caused a state of emotions. The great terrible gulping sobs locked in her chest were begging to come out. Margaret placed her hands over her eyes and shook her head back and forth, firmly holding back the tears of grief and confusion. Feeling the worst was about to come, Margaret quickly ran back towards the truck. She tore into the woods, trying to suppress the inevitable breakdown which had been held tightly in place by years of being a responsible mother, loving daughter, and devoted friend. The composure she had tried so hard to sustain snapped like a fragile twig. She ran towards the metal enclosure, tears blinding her steps. Her body felt weightless as her foot caught the decomposing log, making her fall forward. The hard fall jolted the deep subconscious memory of the day she first met him.

Chapter 4

December 14, 1962 was a chilly early winter's day. Margaret was spending her first year after high school graduation staying home with her father, hoping to decide which college to attend. There was an arts college in Greenville that was the closest to home. The thought of leaving her father alone was more than she could deal with. The two had taken care of each other since her mother's death.

Margaret felt she didn't really need college. She told her dad what she really wanted was to stay home close to Lake Mattamuskeet and paint, but she knew he didn't believe her. The college brochures in the mailbox told him there was a possibility Margaret was entertaining other ideas, but Thomas couldn't persuade his stubborn daughter to pursue her dreams of attending college. He reiterated to Margaret that he would be okay alone on the farm, but Margaret's argument was that she was already making a good living painting the wildlife at Lake Mattamuskeet, and while the getting was still good, she would continue to take advantage of this opportunity to sell her paintings to those who visited Mattamuskeet Lodge. Ever since Margaret was fourteen, many of her paintings had hung on the walls there, fetching more money than she had ever dreamed. The Lodge keeper, Lawrence Davenport, got a commission for each painting sold. He told Margaret that the hunters liked the realistic beauty of the birds she painted, but it was hard for Margaret to understand how they could appreciate something they didn't hesitate to kill.

At nineteen, Margaret liked the independence to do the things she loved, like painting. She helped her dad around the farm, but when the birds migrated to Lake Mattamuskeet, she spent every possible moment in the tree stand.

Margaret stared out into the woods, hesitating before she picked up her paint brush to paint, she wanted to fully take in the scene in front of her - woodlands and fringed marshes further out, and in the foreground a low mist enshrouding the swans, which were tightly huddled together in the shallow pool, protecting each other from the blast of a shotgun. The private land was off limits to the hunters. Over the years the wooded area surrounding them had become a safe haven for many different species of waterfowl.

Margaret slid on her fingerless gloves. The missing finger tips allowed her to securely hold the paint brush, while still keeping the rest of her hands warm. Looking out, she took a few moments to rest her eyes on the breath-taking scene before her and then, as though possessed, the canvas began to come alive with a mixture of colors. The images before her slowly took form, beginning with the delicacy of each feather. The swans' long necks were distinguished by a thin salmon-pink streak running along the mouth line. The careful stroke of her brush's tip lined the black bill with such ease the magnificent bird almost came alive.

Margaret concentrated on the glide of her brush, carefully lining the dark eyes and adding the touch that almost brought life into the feathery creature. She stared deeply into the painting, steadying the yellow-tipped bristles to lightly add the final touch to the swan. Margaret slid the yellow paint in front of the eye to reveal its breed from the many other breeds of swans that frequented the marshlands. Leaning back, Margaret smiled, satisfied, as she stared at the painting. She then dipped the bristle's tip in black paint to touch up around the eyes, concentrating so deeply she could almost feel a slight breeze as she imagined the painted feathery creature flapping its wings.

A smile of satisfaction beamed across Margaret's face. Leaning back, as she was reaching for another canvas, the sky exploded with feathers. The loud sound shook her off the stool as the waterfowl beat the air with their wings, struggling towards a safer direction, frantically trying to get away from the noise they feared the most. Birds took to the air, floating upward, whirling around in small spirals that became larger and larger, until the sky was filled with the feathery creatures' deafening high-pitched screams.

Margaret stood looking back towards where she had parked, when she heard another blast, louder and even closer than before. Looking behind her, she saw something moving in the brush, and as she looked closer she could see the muzzle of a shotgun smoking. The next shot left the long barrel, hitting another bird. Margaret grabbed her shotgun and quickly climbed out of the tree.

Margaret quietly positioned herself, closing her left eye. She looked right down the barrel, aligning for a shot to the base of the skull. She stood behind the man as he was about to take another shot. Holding the shotgun steady, she kept her sight, standing firm. The anger in her voice shook her. "Put down the gun before I blow you away."

The man watched his target fly away, hesitating before bringing the barrel of the shotgun down. Margaret was too angry to be scared. Breathing hard, she stood her ground as she kept her eye on the man. He wore a brown wool herringbone sport coat with knickers, and waders like none she had ever seen the locals wear. With his finger off the trigger, he hesitated before asking, "Ma'am, can you tell me what your problem is? And please, will you put down that shotgun? You're making me nervous."

Margaret flinched a little, but continued to stare at him, her eyes determined, her mouth set in a firm line. She tried to keep her voice calm. Looking at the dead birds, Margaret wasn't ready to put down the gun. She was both angry and saddened at their vulnerability to these predators that so frequented the area to stalk and kill these beautiful creatures. Feeling her face flushed with anger, she asked, "What are you doing here?"

The man could obviously hear how upset she was, and he hesitated before replying. "I'm staying at the Mattamuskeet Lodge with some friends. This morning we all started bird hunting." Speaking quickly, he stopped to take in a deep breath before continuing, "I somehow got separated from them and just decided to continue hunting, hoping to meet up with them eventually. I don't know what I've done to deserve a gun to my head."

Margaret didn't know whether to believe him or not, but she did know by his attire that he wasn't one of the locals, and he did have a strange but pronounce way of saying his words. She took in a deep breath, continuing to grip the gun tightly. Looking down, she noticed his pant legs were shaking as if he was scared she might shoot if he moved. A sense of relief washed over his face when he saw the gun's barrel swing around to point in the opposite direction.

Hoping it was safe, he hesitated before slowly turning to see the fair-haired beauty before him. She wore a hat, and in its faded letters he could make out a possible G or B, but not enough to form any recognition of a word. Her worn, oversize jacket gave him no indication of her size. For a second he was lost in the emerald eyes staring back at him. It wasn't that her features were perfect, but she had a sensuality that made him want to kiss her without ever stopping to ask her name. Even with her face filled with anger, he thought she was the most beautiful woman he had ever seen. Her eyes coldly stared back at him, darkened by anger, and he quickly snapped out of his trance.

Realizing what had just happened, his demeanor changed. Margaret struggled to hold her stance. She drew in a deep agitated breath as she stared at the dead birds.

The emotions that played over her face ranged from anger to sadness. Tears she refused to shed burned hot behind her lids. She traded the harsh tone in her voice for a quiet whisper, saying, "This is private property. It's owned by my father, who is a local farmer."

His blue eyes stared intently back at her. He felt he hadn't done anything wrong. He couldn't understand how killing three birds could make someone so angry. Choosing his words carefully, he said, "I apologize; I didn't know. I got the impression from the Lodge keeper that we could hunt on all the land surrounding the lake." Nervously catching his breath, he paused before speaking, "He didn't say anything about private property. Again, I am sorry." He tried to calm her by grabbing her arm, further saying, "Isn't bird hunting why people come to Lake Mattamuskeet?"

Now she was furious. She wrenched her arm away from him, reaching out to slap him hard across the face. He didn't even flinch, though he wanted to defend himself as he watched the anger stream down her face. Her reaction made him forget all about his earlier thoughts. All he could do was apologize again as she dried her tears. It was at that moment that he began to feel she would be okay, and all he really wanted to do was get out of there.

Hoping he wouldn't get shot in the back, he quickly turned to hike back to the Lodge. Margaret watched him for a second, knowing he would never find his way back. Really she didn't care if he didn't, but before she knew it, she heard herself shouting at him, hoping to capture his attention. "Hey! It's a long walk, and with these short winter days it'll be dark soon. I'll give you a ride. Help me get the birds so I can carry them back to the farm to bury."

He didn't know what would happen next, but the tone of her voice made him stop in place. He turned on command, and before he realized it he had walked down to the water's edge with her to retrieve the dead birds. She handed him two of the birds while she took one. Walking, she continued to scold him. "You killed three Canada Geese! These birds mate for life until one dies. The surviving bird often will not mate again for some years, or even for its entire life! See? You have killed three, leaving one without a mate. It's probably the one over there still honking."

John stared straight down, his blue eyes glazed over by the guilt he felt from the intentional killings of these birds. Listening to Margaret persecute him over and over, he now wished he had hightailed it out of there. The plump geese slowed down his stride, and the lone goose began chasing after him, nipping at his pant leg, hoping he would drop its mate. Margaret looked over at John being physically abused by the goose and hoped he now realized the importance of these creatures, how they reacted like humans whenever they needed to defend themselves and their loved ones.

Margaret's sudden silence caused John to turn towards her. Catching Margaret looking at him with an unusual smirk on her face made his look of frustration quickly give way to a cold stare, his angular jaw clenching as he wondered why he was doing this for someone who obviously would never give up taunting him.

Margaret wanted to look away from him, but his wavy brown hair was losing its hold in the damp air, a loose curl dangling over his right eye. Margaret couldn't help but think how different he looked from the local men.

It was hard listening to the high-pitched sound following them. Both carried the birds to the truck as quickly as possible and put them in the truck's bed. Margaret looked back towards the water. "If you don't mind helping me, I've got a few more things to get." The hunter felt like saying "no," but instead he reluctantly followed Margaret, hoping his help would quickly get them out of there.

Margaret stopped at a tree and stared at him. "Just stay there until I lower the bucket, then remove the items. I've got about two loads." He stood silent as he watched the leather boots positioning their footing on the narrow wooden steps, climbing the tree with such ease. Margaret grabbed a branch to pull herself up to the wooden landing, where she filled a large wash tub with items before lowering it down. He took the items out, then hoisted the bucket back up.

When Margaret lowered the final load, something caught his eye. He reached for the canvas, its beauty and realism startling him. Staring up at her, now he knew why she felt so much anger and sadness towards him. He stared at the painting with a sense of unintentional guilt; its beauty made him speechless. The feathered birds had obviously been passionately captured by a gifted artist.

Embarrassed at what he had done, he could barely look at Margaret as he handed her the painting. Margaret grabbed the painting, and he followed as she quickly walked to the truck. She loaded everything in the back except the painting. Margaret looked up into the sky. The waterfowl had begun to flutter downward in crisscrossing spirals. They noisily rearranged themselves in the cove to feed again, only a few hundred yards from where they'd started. Driving away, they sat quietly, watching the bird flapping its wings for its mate.

The drive to the Lodge was an endless painful silence. Margaret turned down the dirt road, saying nothing as the truck approached the Lodge. John turned to ask if she needed help burying the birds.

"I don't need your help." Her eyes were cold as she stared ahead.

When the truck came to a stop, John quickly reached for the shotgun before getting out. Looking back at her, he felt a genuine pang of sadness. He said, "Again, I would like to say I'm sorry. And for what it's worth, introduce myself. I'm John Ashton." She turned to him with a tired smile, and for an instant he wanted to reach out and touch her.

Margaret nodded, then quickly drove off, but her curiosity slowed down her speed as she watched him in the rearview mirror, still standing in the same spot. He was tall, a handsome man with broad shoulders and deep blue eyes. She tried to study him objectively, but all she could see were the killings. Hesitating before the truck's wheels turned towards home, she looked over her shoulders at the dead birds. Her heart ached for the others frightened away by the gunshots.

Margaret grabbed the shovel from the barn, then hopped back into the truck and pressed down on the clutch, roughly changing gears. She drove to an area of the land designated as the "Farm Cemetery," where they buried wildlife and farm animals. The latest was their dog, Bonner, who had died of old age.

Margaret grabbed the shovel from the bed of the truck. She struggled to dig holes deep enough to bury the birds, pausing only a few times to take a breath from the exhausting work. Her adrenaline kept her relentlessly digging, until her frustrations had all three birds buried quicker than she'd realized.

Looking around, Margaret found three rocks and cleaned them off with her painting rag. Taking a paint brush and dipping its tip in the brown paint, Margaret quickly outlined a goose on each one, then filled in the images to mark each bird. Tired, it was all Margaret could do to turn the ignition, put the truck in gear and drive towards the farmhouse. The distant grey clouds made the sky look threatening and angry. Margaret pressed down on the gas, driving faster towards the house. Hoping to beat the storm, Margaret quickly unloaded the truck and went inside to start supper. She wasn't very hungry, but needed to make sure her father had a hot meal.

In the dim light of the kitchen, Margaret washed the delicate gloves that had been hand knitted by Lillian, then placed them on the backside of the chair closest to the heat. The brown wool had been sheered from one of the four sheep raised on the Rogers' farm. Lillian loomed and dyed her own wool for knitting. She had knit the gloves with the fingertips missing, knowing that Margaret usually cut hers to allow her to firmly hold her brush.

The stoked wood stove in the corner of the room was filled with oak wood, warming everything in the kitchen. The kettle filled with cold water had already begun hissing from the intense heat. A cup of coffee grounds quickly dissolved into the boiling water still bubbling inside Margaret's cup. She wiped a coffee stain from underneath the coffee cup. The cup's warmth helped soothe the tension of the hectic day. Across the field, the distant sound of a goose could be heard; Margaret wondered about the lone goose left calling for its mate.

Staring out the window, she looked for any signs of dust from a tractor tilling up land, but only saw the storm's winds stirring up the dusty fields. The field stretched far, each row filled with dark soil rich enough to support almost any crop. She could hear the wind blowing, making the barn door pound, opening and shutting as air was pulled through the gaps between the wooden slats. A rare December thunderstorm was brewing from the cold and warm air colliding. The air was heavy and metallic. Margaret hated thunderstorms.

The distant rumble hurried her attempts to finish her chores. She jumped as lightning flashed.

A bolt of lightning split the sky as she stepped outside to latch the barn door. She could hear the drone of her father's voice, feel him grab her arm and pull her back inside the kitchen. "I got it Margaret." She stared out into the storm, her eyes wide and glassy, watching her father firmly holding his cap down as the wind tugged on the lightweight fabric. Her heart pounded as she watched him run across the yard towards the barn. Her breathing came in short breaths as the storm grew louder.

As a child, Margaret had been afraid of lightning. The electrical charge streaking across the sky reminded her of the night her mother had died. The weeks after her death, Margaret had slept with her head on her mother's pink scarf; the sweet odor of perfume helped soothe her to sleep.

After bolting the door shut, Thomas quickly started back, reaching the kitchen door just before the rains started. The two of them stood in the doorway a moment, watching the cloud burst pour in gusty sweeps over the ground. Margaret took Thomas's coat to securely hang it on the metal hook, and then walked over to the stove to finish their supper.

He saw the troubled look in her eyes, the tense lines of strain in her face. Thomas said, "Honey, the storms about over." He reached over to touch her shoulder, saying, "How was your day?"

Margaret stared down into the pot. His caring words brought tears to her eyes. Trying to keep her composure, she smiled, shaking her head up and down. "It was good, Dad. I painted most of the day. How was yours?" Margaret could barely get the words out before the tears came pouring down her cheeks, the small drops landing on the dish towel. Her heart saddened by what had happened, she turned around and threw her arms around her dad's neck.

He embraced her while she cried. "Margaret, are you okay? Did something bad happen? Please dear, tell me what's wrong."

Margaret tried to wipe the tears away, but his gentle voice just made them flow harder. Holding her, he pleaded for her to tell him what happened. Since his wife had died, Thomas felt compelled to protect his daughter from any harm. Sometimes Margaret felt suffocated by her dad's soft words. She pulled away from his embrace, wiping her tears with the apron wrapped around her waist. She hesitated before reaching in the oven to take out the biscuits. Margaret placed the pan on the stove top and grabbed the container of tea, pouring them both a glass.

Thomas was worried something terrible had happened. "Margaret? Darling, what's wrong?" There were tears still trembling in her eyes and she didn't even know where to begin. The story of what had happened was harder to tell than Margaret realized, but she managed to finally tell Thomas what had happened in the woods. Telling him what happened brought some sense of relief, but reliving the moment again was heartbreaking. Thomas reached for her hand, while using his free hand to wipe away her tears. He too, was saddened by the killings, and promised he would go to the Lodge tomorrow to speak with Lawrence.

Margaret caught her breath and dried her eyes with her napkin. She sat down at the table, one leg curled under her, and pulled back the strands of hair that had fallen over her face. Reaching back for her dad's hand, she said, "No dad, please don't say anything. I'll be okay."

After giving her a kiss on the forehead, her father sat down with her at the table to eat supper.

Chapter 5

A fter the storm, Thomas Windley went about his business, unloading the trailer attached to the Farmall tractor. As he pulled the tractor into the barn he worried about Margaret. Since his wife Jacqueline had passed away, he'd tried to help Margaret understand that life around them was delicate; the land, waterfowl and people made up the community of New Holland, but Lake Mattamuskeet gave life to a community limited by their source of income. Most hunters spent a lot of money to pursue their sport by hunting in the area. Many stayed at the Lodge, which employed locals who could not support their families in the winter months when the farming season ended.

As he walked back towards the house, Thomas could see Margaret through the kitchen window washing the dishes. She reminded him of how Jacqueline had loved keeping house and had taken such good care of Margaret; she took pride in being a wife and mother. Her death had come from a lightning strike during a storm as she ran out to put the horses in the barn. He remembered the night as though it were yesterday. The strike had been hard and strong; it struck the big oak tree, catching up with Jacqueline as she ran towards the barn. Her lifeless body had been soaked from the pouring rain until Thomas arrived home. It had been the first thing he saw as he drove up to the house, the truck's high beams spotlighting Margaret in a fetal position, holding tightly to her mother's body.

Every night thereafter Margaret had slept wrapped up in her mother's perfumed scarf. When the scent had seemed to fade, Thomas sprayed the honeysuckle mist on the soft wool, until the one morning the unwrapped scarf was left alone on the floor. Thomas Windley couldn't bear the loss of his wife, yet he kept busy farming. He had been grateful to Lillian Rogers for helping him care for Margaret during those difficult days. It was Lillian who had shown Margaret how to paint, helping her channel through those tragic emotions of her mother's death.

Thomas hugged his daughter goodnight, and then both walked down opposite ends of the hall toward their rooms. Lying quietly in her bed, Margaret could hear the waterfowl coming from the water's edge, each playing their own unique instrument. As she rolled on her side, Margaret heard a honking noise in the distance. She tried not to think about the lone bird flying overhead, possibly looking for its mate buried just beyond the field.

The next morning, the sound of the birds' music wasn't enough to motivate Margaret to answer their calls. It was all she could do to crawl out of bed to wash her face. As she brushed her hair into a ponytail all she could think of was yesterday's killing, and that she hadn't been able to protect the birds from the hunter. Putting on her shoes, she heard her dad calling up the stairs.

"Margaret, there is a young man here to see you."

Grabbing her coat, she hollered back, "Tell Henry I will be right down." Henry always came around unexpectedly.

Grabbing her gloves, she quickly exited the room and ran down the stairs. Reaching the bottom step, she skidded to a stop, speechless at the sight standing before her. It was the hunter. John Ashton. Both stared at each other; Margaret couldn't believe her eyes.

"What are you doing here?" she gasped. "I think I've seen enough of you. Why don't you leave?" Before he could answer, Margaret's dad told her to apologize to Mr. Ashton. Furious, Margaret turned to look at her dad.

"Don't think I'll be apologizing to Mr. Ashton today, tomorrow, or ever! I believe I'm the one who deserves an apology."

John Ashton reached for the shotgun he had mistakenly taken the day Margaret dropped him off at the Lodge. "Here Ms. Windley, this shotgun belongs to you. I believe you have my shotgun."

Margaret stared at the gun, thinking how that day her emotions had kept her from noticing whose shotgun was left in the truck. As she looked at his face, his sincere demeanor made her speechless. Margaret stood quietly, feeling a little uncomfortable as her father reached for the shotgun. Thomas Windley told John to sit tight, he would run out to the truck to get his shotgun. Before leaving, he looked at Margaret, saying, "Margaret Ann, how about offering Mr. Ashton something to drink."

Margaret sighed, knowing her dad was losing his patience with her when he called her Margaret Ann. Forcing a smile she asked, "Would you like something to drink?"

Before John could say yes, he watched her turn to walk towards the kitchen. He waited quietly as she poured him a glass of sweet tea. Reaching for the glass, he politely said "Thanks."

Taking a sip, John hesitated before speaking, "Hey, I'd like to apologize again for killing the birds. I am truly sorry, and have decided not to hunt during the remainder of my stay here. Also, I saw your paintings hanging on the walls in the Lodge. You're a very talented painter. I was looking at buying a couple of them." He stared at her, waiting for a response as he continued sipping the tea.

With her back towards him, she reached for a dish towel to wipe the surface, responding, "You'd need to see the Lodge keeper. I don't have anything to do with any of that, I just paint. What else, Mr. Ashton?"

Before he could respond, Thomas walked in with the shotgun. "Here you go Mr. Ashton, sorry for the inconvenience." John put down the glass and grabbed the shotgun. Both he and Thomas walked towards the front door, chatting on the way.

Margaret became restless when their conversation grew longer than she wanted it to. Grabbing a couple of ham biscuits her dad had fixed earlier, Margaret began to pack herself a lunch. She became frustrated once she realized she was late for the trip to the lake. There were only a few weeks left before the birds migrated elsewhere.

Margaret walked out to the truck and loaded everything in the front seat. Realizing she'd forgotten her gloves, she ran back into the house. After grabbing them, she was about to run out the door when her dad called her back.

"Hey, Margaret, how about giving John a ride back to the Lodge?"

In an objecting tone, Margaret shouted back, "I've already put everything in the front seat, Dad. There's no room! I'm running late, I need to go!"

Before he could answer, she was already backing the truck out and heading towards the road. Looking in the mirror, she could see John waving at her dad and walking in her direction. As she was about to turn she thought about something her dad always said: "It is easier to forget than to forgive." But Margaret couldn't understand how you could forgive if you could never forget something so tragic. Margaret settled for a more realistic reason for giving John a ride, reminding herself that last night's storm had caused freezing temperatures, making the early morning rain turn to a light snow. Margaret brought the truck to a halt and moved the canvases occupying the passenger seat and waited for John to catch up to the truck.

John watched the brake lights come on, as if she had just thought of something she'd forgotten. When he walked up beside her, she looked a little startled and then quietly said, "Get in, I'll give you a ride." He jumped into the truck.

John stared at Margaret longer than he should, his consciousness filling with the urge to say something. Instead, he opted for silence and turned to stare ahead at the road. They sat so quietly he could hear her softly breathing. After turning down the path, he felt disappointed when they approached the Lodge, for he longed to spend more time with her.

As he reached for the door handle, he thought quickly and stared back at her excitedly, saying, "Hey, I'd like to show you which paintings I would like to buy."

Margaret tried to feign the same excitement. Letting out a deep sigh, she grabbed the door handle. Once inside the Lodge, she looked around as he pointed out the Tundra Swans paired together on the canvas.

Margaret turned and glared at him, bluntly saying, "After what happened I'm surprised you like this one." The words were no sooner out of her mouth than she wished she could snatch them back.

Before he could answer, a deep voice could be heard coming down the hall behind them. "Margaret, what brings you here? I never get to see you! Thomas always brings all your paintings. Whatever it is, I'm glad you came. I've got some things to go over with you."

Mr. Davenport walked up and stood behind John. The jolly white-haired, heavy set man's waist line was more noticeable with his heavily starched shirt tucked into his dark wool pants. Margaret smiled and nudging past John, she gave the old man a hug.

"Lawrence, I've been busy painting, trying to capture all this beauty here at Lake Mattamuskeet! You know I don't approve of hunting, so I don't come around here much, but I like what you all have done to the Lodge."

Quickly she turned around, but hesitated before walking into the large room. "I forgot how big that fireplace is. And so beautifully decorated! Wow, look at the tree….. It's huge."

Walking closer, Margaret paraded around the Christmas tree, smiling. "I recognize these decorations! Lillian and I painted them." She reached for the wooden Tundra Swan painted white, loosely hanging by a string. Turning around, she said, "Wow, they turned out really good."

Margaret walked to the middle of the room and twirled around, trying to take in the large room. She couldn't help but notice all the stuffed birds looking as real as the day they were killed, each stuffed to simulate a permanent poise. The massive furniture was welcoming, making it feel cozy. Margaret looked at all the paintings surrounding the room, all by the same artist – herself. It was an awesome feeling seeing all her paintings hanging in the large room; this was the first time she'd actually seen them hanging inside the Lodge. Her father always delivered her paintings, and each time he came home to tell his daughter how beautiful they looked on display, and that she needed to go see them for herself, yet each time Margaret refused to go to the hunting Lodge. Over the years she had sold many to the hunters who frequented the Lodge. Margaret had also given several to Mr. Davenport to permanently hang on the walls, hoping the waterfowl on canvas would somehow change the way the gun-carrying visitors felt about killing the delicate creatures.

Mr. Davenport's voice broke her trance. "Hey Margaret, why don't you come to the annual Christmas Ball next Saturday? Many locals will be attending. There will be a band, lots of food, and of course a fundraiser to raise money for a bird refuge. Hopefully, one day this whole area will become a refuge, something I know you would wholeheartedly support."

Margaret smiled, liking what she heard as she thought of her own personal commitment to give thirty percent from the sale of every painting she sold for waterfowl conservation. The area temporarily housed rare species of waterfowl that migrated to Lake Mattamuskeet, which provided a temporary home to many who spent their winters in the thicket surrounding the lake. Unfortunately, the area had become a magnet for many hunters, who spent weeks killing these beautiful creatures. Margaret would do anything to protect the wildlife at Lake Mattamuskeet.

"Lawrence, you know I might take you up on that offer, but only if you let me auction off my prize painting."

The "prize painting" had been produced during a rare moment when unexpectedly, possibly from a severe storm, a handful of Black Swans, native to Australia, found refuge on Lake Mattamuskeet. Black swans do not migrate, but are nomadic, following food sources and adequate water. These had found those necessities for survival in the deep cove. Most likely the swans had lived in an aviary on the East Coast; the storm must have damaged their habitat. Margaret had watched for months as they laid eggs and hatched their young, keeping it a secret since she didn't want the locals to stampede to the area. She had only told her father and Lillian. Margaret had spent weeks painting the beautiful birds and their young. She'd been keeping the painting to herself, hoping that one year the birds would return to Lake Mattamuskeet. By now, Margaret thought it was time to unveil this rare moment captured on canvas.

It was getting late. Saying her good-byes, Margaret squeezed past the two standing in the doorway. Walking down the steps, she overheard John Ashton telling Lawrence he would be leaving on Monday - his father was expecting him back in New York. He repeated the words as she walked past them without expression. Margaret felt the words grab her heart. Feeling something she had never felt before, she walked faster, not wanting John to see the anxiety, she could all but hide on her face. As she reached the truck, Margaret caught a quick glimpse of John. After realizing she'd looked at him longer than she should, she quickly jumped in the driver's side.

Margaret tried to start the truck, but it wouldn't turn-over. Desperately, she kept pumping the gas pedal, flooding the engine, stopping only when she could smell the strong odor of gasoline. Frustrated, Margaret slowed her thoughts enough to keep her foot off the pedal. She turned to see John Ashton staring at her. His laughter changed to a compassionate smile when he saw the frustration in her eyes.

Opening the driver door, he insisted, "Let me help you out Margaret. Move over."

She hesitated before sliding across to the passenger side. As he got in, his hand slid across her leg. Realizing this, he quickly reached for the ignition. He turned the ignition switch, to no avail. Looking back at her, their eyes met and as he turned the key, the engine roared to life.

Before he could say anything, Margaret said, "Thanks Mr. Ashton, but I've got to go. I'm already late. I should have been painting an hour ago."

Hesitating for a moment, sensing her impatience, John quickly asked if she would have dinner with him tomorrow tonight. Stunned, she laughed at the question, and he noticed her long, graceful neck.

When she realized he was serious, Margaret stopped laughing. She didn't want to sound too eager, but hesitantly said, "I don't know, I've got to get going. It may be late before I finish painting."

John smiled, drawing on his law studies for persuasiveness. "Margaret, I really owe you for my behavior. Please let me buy you dinner Sunday night. The special at the Lodge is steak, no waterfowl."

His eyes looked directly at her, and she felt something jump inside. The only thing Margaret could conclude was that John Ashton had somehow drawn her in by catching her off guard. Listening to the engine idling, John patiently waited for an answer, knowing she was anxious to get going. Margaret quickly gave it the gas and dusted off Mr. Ashton, who never moved, but stood in the same place as she drove away, as if he was still waiting for her answer.

Chapter 6

M aking the turn towards the water's edge, Margaret felt a twinge of apprehension, but managed to finally slow her thoughts of John Ashton. She smiled, sensing an unusual feeling of anticipation. Other than Henry, she had never been asked out on a date. Henry was her closest male friend, but other than good friends Margaret did not feel attracted to Henry. Unfortunately, Henry seemed to want something more than just friendship.

As she sat down to paint the beauty staged before her, she whispered to herself, "God thank you for this breathtaking day."

Margaret's mind finally caught up with the brush strokes, slowing down enough to intricately paint each feather of the Trumpeter Swans landing on the water, their wings making a raspy noise behind their hollow-sounding honking. The swans hovered together on the water's edge, as if hoping to protect themselves from the wrath of a hunter. The thought of auctioning off many of her paintings gave Margaret enthusiasm to concentrate on each detail of the scenery, making sure each stroke realistically captured the essence of these beautiful creatures.

Hours passed before Margaret completed the painting. It depicted a pool of Trumpeter Swans in the tiny cove. As if the birds knew this was a safe place, the cove was heavily populated with waterfowl. An overabundance of white swans bunching together like a blanket of snow caught her eye. Staring beyond them, Margaret noticed a couple of swans kissing, their long necks and breasts connecting forming the shape of a heart. Margaret had a painting hanging at the Lodge that showed this affectionate poise.

The shorter winter days soon had Margaret packing. She loaded the truck parked under the big oak tree. Feeling the cold wind, she cranked the truck and turned on the heater to warm the inside. She stepped out of the truck to finish loading when a horrible sound came from the water's edge. The excruciating high-pitched noise made her body rigid, her legs stalling for a brief moment before grabbing the shotgun and running towards the lake. The intense sound had her tearing through the thicket, the cold air burning her nostrils. She feared another hunter had injured one of the waterfowl. In her panic, she ran out onto the ice before she realized she had gotten so close to the water's edge. Her feet pounded on the rim of ice around the lake, cracking the thin surface.

The frigid waters of the lake gave way to Margaret's fall. The shotgun left her grip. She looked down in terror, eyes following the sinking shotgun. Instinctively she reached out to catch hold of the gun, but it was sinking too fast. Losing sight of the gun, Margaret rolled face up, trying to swim up through the murkiness. Her mind was awash with images of her mother, smiling as she reached for her daughter.

A white hand, blurred by the cloudy waters, descended, and Margaret grabbed on. A firm grip pulled her back towards the surface, the light filtering through the water outlining the face of someone she knew. Reaching the surface, Margaret gulped in air, then began coughing uncontrollably, her body convulsing from the freezing temperatures. The flapping white wings all around her made the temperature feel even colder.

John wrapped the dry jacket around her shoulders and pulled her closer towards his chest, tightly holding her. Margaret's cries further agitated the waterfowl, causing them to slap their wings and feet in unison as they pounded along the water's surface, struggling to get airborne.

Margaret looked at John, her eyes filled with fear. The smell of his skin calmed her cries, making her feel protected. The cold water soaked through her clothes, clinging to her skin and making her body shiver. As though she were a rag doll, he scooped her up and quickly carried her to the warm truck.

Margaret held tightly to the one person she had distrusted the most. Sobbing, she said, "Thank you John. I'm sorry for my mean words."

John held Margaret tightly, repeatedly telling her she was safe now, soothing her sobs to quiet sniffles. Clutching him tightly, Margaret's thoughts escaped through her trembling lips. "John, you saved my life. What made you come back here?"

Looking down, his blue eyes seem to resonate nothing but kindness. John wiped away her tears, softly telling Margaret what had brought him back to the one place he promised her he would never again return. John kept his arms around her protectively. His voice was low and filled with emotion. "Margaret, when I drove up you were reaching inside the truck for the shotgun and taking off running towards the lake. I could see the panic in your face, so I jumped out of the truck and chased after you towards the sound. When I lost sight of you I realized you must have fallen in. When I got to the lake, I could see your hand coming out of the lake, and I reached for it."

John's explanation had Margaret sitting up and staring back at John. "I could have died if you hadn't come back. Even though the depth of the water is no more than a few feet, by the time I found my way through the murky water the frigid temperatures would have gotten me first." Margaret realized fate had intervened once again with the return of the shotgun.

Looking at John, her thoughts made her smile. "You took my shotgun so you could bring it to me." Still smiling, Margaret suddenly became aware of something. "Hey John, so if you have my shotgun then I must have yours."

Smiling sheepishly, John said, "I just couldn't take the chance of not seeing you again. I borrowed Lawrence's truck to bring you back your shotgun, but hoped to persuade you to have dinner with me." Margaret laughed, making John shout, "What! Okay, I apologize for taking your damn gun Margaret, but now we're even."

Margaret was feeling a whole lot better now. Her lips tightly pulled together and pushed outward like she was about to plant a kiss on his lips. Her intent stare made him wonder for a second if she would, but instead she placed her hand on his shoulder, saying, "Well John, I'm sorry to tell you this, but I was holding onto your gun when I fell through the ice. It's now at the bottom of the lake." For a second it had not registered, then before he realized it the two of them began laughing.

John stopped, looking seriously at Margaret and pushing the wet strands of hair away from her face. He quietly whispered, "That's okay. I can replace the shotgun, but not you, Margaret. You are a rarity. How about it Margaret, have dinner with me?"

Margaret couldn't resist his sincere approach. She relinquished her stubbornness to accept John's request, saying, "Only if I can cook!" Margaret further explained how she needed to make sure her dad had a home-cooked meal at night. John suddenly realized he was seeing a side of Margaret he had never seen. It was at that moment that he knew he was in trouble.

Even though John insisted on driving Margaret home, she emphatically positioned herself in the driver seat, telling him she was perfectly okay to drive herself home. John reached for the passenger door handle and shook his head, saying, "You sure are a stubborn woman, Margaret Windley! What time do you want me there tomorrow night?"

Margaret, still wearing his jacket, turned to face him, grinning at his comment. "I like to have dinner ready about 6:00. John, let's not mention anything about what happened today. My dad will just start to worry about me every time I come to the lake."

Understandingly, John shook his head up and down, knowing he would probably be the one to worry about her now. As he started up Lawrence's truck, he motioned for Margaret to go first. She put the truck in gear. Moving forward, he waved as she drove away.

Chapter 7

Two cups of vegetables, roast, oil, add a tablespoon of flour… Add a cup of water, brown the roast on both sides, put it all in a deep pan in the oven at 350 degrees for one hour…

Upstairs, Margaret started a bath. She stood in front of the mirror to undress, staring at her body. Lifting her long slender legs, she slipped one then the other into the bath water. Feeling the heat sink into her skin, she gasped from the temperature as she submersed her body into the hot water. Margaret lay quietly in the bathtub, listening to the drip drip of the faucet. Reaching for the soap, Margaret lathered her body and then pulled the plug. She stood up to shower off the soapy film.

As she dried off, she could hear her dad shouting up the stairs. "Goodness Margaret, what is that wonderful smell? Is that pot roast?"

Margaret was in such a rush to paint when church let out that she had forgotten to tell her dad they had company coming over for dinner. An hour beforehand, she suddenly remembered. "Dad, John Ashton will be here in an hour for dinner."

There was a long silence, and then she heard, "Okay, but Margaret, I can't stay for dinner. I promised some of the local farmers we would meet tonight about the problems we're having with irrigating our crops."

Margaret knew the government didn't like the local farmers using the lake during the hot summer months for irrigation, but without it the farmers' crops wouldn't survive. Many farmers used no fertilizer to grow their crops - the land surrounding the lake was rich with minerals. Hyde County received an average of only 60 inches of rainfall a year, and even though Lake Mattamuskeet was the largest natural lake in North Carolina, the farmers still relied on its use for irrigating their crops. Margaret wanted her dad to stay, but she knew the local farmers relied on him to be their voice. He had the ability to communicate what they all felt was needed to resolve the issue.

As Margaret stared out her bedroom window, the coastal clouds passed before the late-afternoon sun, suddenly muting the fiery colors and giving promise to an early-evening drizzle. Reaching inside her closet for the black dress, she hesitated, choosing instead the blue knit dress she'd purchased in Greenville. She sprayed her perfume sparingly - one last wisp, and then she slipped on the dress. Looking in the mirror, she realized she had to do something about her long unruly hair. Grabbing a handful of hairpins, she began to pin up her hair.

Characteristically, she lacked a painted look. Instead, Margaret liked to look natural. She felt colors should only be applied on a canvas, not a woman's face. So, she only sponged a little rouge on her cheeks. She couldn't remember where she had left her black shoes. She searched through the closet, saying to herself, "Shoes, shoes, shoes; where are they?" Suddenly she remembered that while in a hurry to paint, she had absently kicked them off after church. Bending down and looking under the bed, she spotted one, then the other.

At exactly five-thirty Margaret rushed down the stairs, almost tripping on the last step and catching the stair rail as her left leg slid out from underneath her. She laughed, the excitement becoming more than she was used to. Slowing down and trying to calm herself, she took in a deep breath and carefully walked into the dining room. She pulled out the good china her mother had inherited from her grandmother.

The hand-painted china came from her mother's family, who had immigrated to the area from Ohio in 1918, when New Holland Farms sold the lake property to another group from Ohio. This particular area was where her grandfather had come to help engineer pumping out Lake Mattamuskeet, and it was where her mother had begun dating a man she could not leave. When her mother's parents had returned back to Ohio, her mother, Jacqueline stayed to marry Thomas Windley. Looking at the hand-painted china setting - two plates, silverware and wine goblets - Margaret couldn't remember the last time they'd used all sixteen pieces. Normally, they were left protected in the china cabinet given to her mother as an anniversary gift from her dad. Quietly shutting the glass door, Margaret rubbed the smooth wood; the handmade cabinet was a work of art by a local carpenter.

Looking at the kitchen clock, she realized she only had about fifteen minutes to get the food prepared. Grabbing the kitchen towel, she opened the oven to check the roast, poking it with a fork. Margaret wasn't the best cook in Hyde County, but Lillian had taught her early in life how to cook the basics. Later she'd started experimenting with many dishes - some good, others bad, but most of the time it was edible. Running around the kitchen, she reached in the oven to take out the biscuits, when she heard a knock at the door.

"John is early," she thought to herself.

Wiping her hands dry on the apron, she reached behind to untie it and left it on the stool. As she rushed towards the door, she stopped in front of the mirror to check her looks. When she opened the door, there he stood, looking better than she had ever seen him. He was wearing clothes like none she had ever seen any man in the area wearing, the paisley open collar shirt, thin striped gray wool trousers and a double- breasted wool jacket to match. And the cologne - the warm spicy scent made her want to stand there awhile and linger in it. When she suddenly realized she was blocking his entrance, she backed up and asked him to come inside.

Stepping in the door, he held out a small bouquet of flowers – roses - and a bottle of wine. His eyes looked directly into hers, making something jolt inside. The eyes, the voice, his smell; all were equally drawing her closer to him; closer to the moment when two people realize they have something magical. Taking in a deep breath, Margaret overheard herself saying, "Wow, you clean up nicely." Realizing what she had just said, she could feel her face flush from embarrassment. Turning, she took the wine bottle to the kitchen as he put his coat on the hook.

The bottle of wine made Margaret nervous. She had only drank wine once before, while attending a wedding at the Lodge.

She really didn't even remember the one glass, but managed to get the bottle open. Returning with two glasses filled to the rim, she handed one to John.

As he looked at her, he couldn't resist saying, "My, you clean up nicely, and smell good too." The two started to laugh, each knowing it was the truth.

John, grabbing the glass, said, "Wow, you got it filled to the rim." He carefully sipped some off the top, careful not to spill any on the furniture. John intently stared at Margaret for any sign of yesterday's accident. Staring back at him, Margaret again thanked John for saving her life. The two laughed at each other's like thoughts.

The living room was dark. As Margaret turned on the lamp, John saw that the room was filled with overlarge pieces of furniture. A small Christmas tree in the corner, filled with wooden ornaments representing the waterfowl of Lake Mattamuskeet, caught his eye. Reaching out, he twirled the string keeping a wooden Tundra Swan airborne.

"I like these, they're so realistic."

Margaret smiled. "These were made by Paul Rogers and painted by me and Lillian Rogers. They own the farm next door to us." She watched his eye movements as he turned to the pictures hung on the flower printed walls.

She saw him smile, and then he looked at her with an amused expression. He couldn't help but notice one of Margaret. Picking up the picture for a closer look, he said, "I like this one of you."

She was barefoot, wearing jeans and a white peasant blouse with the sleeves rolled up and the shirttail out. She was stretched out on the front porch swing at sixteen; the picture had been taken by Henry, who just received the camera for his birthday.

He said, "The light was perfect." His eyes met hers. Breaking their connection, he reached for the glass and followed her to the kitchen where she served their plates.

The two sat, and she said the blessing. Margaret smiled softly, feeling a little awkward about having a man over for dinner. How strange life was. Here he was, and she was having dinner with him; her heart was pounding, and she had to admit, she was excited about it. He was a very attractive man, and there was something different about him.

Margaret took a deep breath, and then suddenly she was looking into those deep blue eyes again. Considering how they met, Margaret would have never expected she would ever feel this way. The silence between them began to feel awkward, and she was struggling for something to say to him.

Looking down as she moved her food around the plate with her fork, Margaret asked, "How much longer will you be staying at the Lodge?" She already knew the answer after overhearing John telling Lawrence he would be leaving Monday, but she was hoping he had changed his plans.

John put his fork down to answer her. "I was thinking Monday, but then someone came along distracting me, clouding my thoughts, and causing me to question my decision to leave. It couldn't have been that deranged woman I met on my first day here at Lake Mattamuskeet. She was so mean, but for some reason I can't get her off my mind. I wonder who she was."

They both laughed. John began speaking about his recent graduation from Harvard Law School, the same school, he told Margaret, his father and grandfather had attended. As he monopolized the conversation, Margaret kept thinking to herself how little she knew about places outside of New Holland. Finally, there was silence as he caught her daydreaming, staring beyond him as though something else had caught her attention. John cleared his throat.

Margaret looked at John. "I heard every word you said, John."

John nodded, "Well, I apparently didn't say anything to capture your attention enough to stay focused on me. You going to eat the rest of your roast?"

Margaret stared down at her plate then looked back at John. "No. You want it?"

"If you don't. This is really good Margaret," John said.

About the time they had finished and cleared everything, Thomas walked into the house, finding the two laughing as they washed dishes. As Thomas stood watching the two clean up the kitchen, he suddenly wondered if he wasn't seeing something special. There was something different about Margaret tonight; she seemed comfortable with John. The two truly complimented each other. From his conversations with Lawrence, Thomas knew John would be leaving next week. Thomas didn't want Margaret to get hurt from someone who planned on returning to New York. Clearing his throat, Thomas walked into the kitchen.

Surprised to see him, Margaret almost dropped the plate she was holding. "Hey daddy, I didn't hear you come in. John and I just finished dinner." She set the plate down on the counter. "We've got plenty left, you want something to eat?"

Thomas grabbed a glass and filled it with water. Taking a swallow, he said, "I will take a couple of sandwiches with me tomorrow; Steve Jessup's wife Melissa fixed us all a spread of food, but not as good as your cooking, Margaret."

Turning to John, he apologized for not being able to join the two for dinner. Gulping down the remainder of the water, he said, "I'm sure the meal was good."

Agreeing with Thomas, John nodded his head, saying, "Thomas, I understand you had some important farming issues to resolve. Let me know if I can help you with any legal issues." Margaret, washing a dish, looked up and smiled at John.

Thomas put the glass next to the sink saying, "Thanks John, let me see how things go with those politicians in Raleigh. I might take you up on that offer." Hesitating before walking out of the room, Thomas turn towards John. "You got a ride back to the Lodge?"

Drying off the dish, John put it on top of the stack before answering. "Yes sir, I've got Lawrence's truck parked on the other side of the house. I didn't want it to be in your way. I told him I wouldn't be long, but he said not to worry. It seems everybody likes Margaret."

They all laughed when Margaret said, "Who, me? Lawrence doesn't know the real me like you John."

Thomas and John talked while Margaret put the china back in the cabinet. She listened as they discussed John's upcoming law exam in New York City that he had to take after the holidays. She could tell her dad really liked John; he was more mature and different from most of the boys in New Holland.

Margaret rarely dated anyone except Henry. Yet, she wouldn't call spending time with Henry dating. He would sometimes stop by to hang around the house with her and Thomas. Or, in the warmer months, they would take the paddle boat out on the lake, sometimes to fish or swim, but mostly just to talk about their dreams. Margaret knew Henry wanted to be more than a friend, but she wasn't ready to settle for something permanent. It made her feel less creative. She hated being labeled someone's girlfriend. Margaret felt there would be limitations on the things she wanted to do, and she didn't want to always feel like she needed to get someone else's approval whenever she decided to spend time with other friends.

Walking into the kitchen, Thomas reminded Margaret he would be attending a farmers' meeting about the water issue in Raleigh tomorrow, but would be back on Thursday. He turned to John, "Several of us will be helping Lawrence get the Lodge ready for Saturday's party. He needs help setting up the tables and chairs. You got any plans?"

John looked at Margaret then Thomas. "No sir. Since I stopped hunting, I'm available all day."

Thomas laughed, saying, "I hope Margaret didn't have anything to do with your decision not to hunt. She can be very influential when she's passionate about something. But don't worry, Margaret will be there too, I volunteered her."

Margaret quickly said, "Dad, I don't have many weeks left before the birds migrate from here. I'll come after lunch." The men in unison laughed at Margaret's quick reaction.

John stood, "I've got to leave before they lock me out of the Lodge, and I know the two of you need to get to bed."

Thomas shook John's hand, apologizing for not being there for dinner, but they all understood. Opening the door, John followed behind Margaret, who walked him to the truck. Stopping, John thanked Margaret for such a wonderful dinner. He hesitated before getting in the truck. Turning to look at Margaret, he quickly asked, "How about spending time with me tomorrow and showing me around the lake?"

Though Margaret was eager to answer, she hesitated for a moment. "I need about two hours tomorrow morning to paint when the sun's coming up. But afterwards…"

John grabbed her hand for one moment and squeezed it hard. He laughed with embarrassment at the look on her face. He wanted to pull her closer to him to kiss her lips, but didn't dare. "I'll see you tomorrow."

Margaret tried to turn away from his stare, but when he reached for her they quickly embraced, the full moon lit-up the moment. Blushing, not wanting her father to see this moment and afraid he would walk outside, Margaret pushed John away.

Feeling a little awkward, Margaret broke away and ran towards the porch. Turning, she hollered, "I'll pick you up at 10:00am; we can get breakfast at Ms. Betty's Cafe."

When she got to the door, Margaret looked distressed; no one had ever touched her as this man had. Shutting the door, she pressed her back up against the closed door, feeling her heart beating fast.

Chapter 8

In the Café the next morning, Ms. Betty - a bleached-blond, slender, quiet-faced woman in her mid-fifties - poured coffee into two cups and placed them on the counter in front of two customers, before moving back to arrange the blueberry muffins in the glass container. The tops of the muffins were embedded with blueberries, and their edges were crispy. Looking inside the case, Margaret pointed to the two larger ones and asked Ms. Betty to wrap them to go. She watched as Ms. Betty carefully wrapped the perfectly shaped muffins, keeping the bag open to put the sausage biscuits in first, not wanting them to crush the baked goods. The door opened and slammed shut, and an elderly couple slowly walked in to seat themselves in a booth. Looking through the window, Margaret could see John seated in the truck patiently waiting for her. "There you go." Ms. Betty handed her the bag of food.

Walking out, Margaret couldn't help but stare at the old man, who scratched at his white beard as his wife fixed him with an annoyed stare. Margaret felt she would not have the endurance to be married to someone, but she knew from last night with John that love was so powerful it could grab your heart without warning, never letting go. Waiting for her to pull away from her stare, a man patiently held the door open for her. Margaret walked through, taking a moment to watch the older woman reach over to remove the crumbs caught in the man's beard. Margaret grinned to herself before thanking the stranger for holding the door open. John jumped out of the truck to grab a coffee and the bag of food from Margaret's grip. Climbing back into the truck, John carefully placed the bag of food on the warm dashboard then grab the other coffee, while Margaret climbed in the truck. As she sipped her coffee, Margaret pointed towards the direction of Lake Mattamuskeet.

On their way to the lake, John drove past the Lodge. He watched a group of young men with their shotguns in their hands on his way past. They stood around a fire burning in a metal cylinder, some with cigarettes drooping from their mouth, spiking their coffee cups with brown liquor, hoping to warm up their insides before going out to guide the hunters at the Lodge.

Margaret spotted Henry amongst them. The two locked eyes, making Margaret uncomfortable. She hesitated before throwing up her hand to wave.

Henry Jessup was a handsome man with tawny hair, a chiseled face, and pewter-gray eyes that made him look older than his twenty years. Farm life had kept his 6'1" stature physically in shape, giving him a good muscular build.

Watching her, John asked, "Who's the guy?"

Looking ahead, Margaret said, "Henry."

John looked over at her for a second, then quietly stared at the road. The road was still dirt, with deep cuts causing the ride to become uncomfortable. It had been awhile since Margaret had traveled down this area of the lake.

The "No Trespassing" sign was now visible, after Clarence Patterson, an attorney from Richmond, Va. purchased the land following the death of the land's owner, Richard Cooley. Cooley's children, Clara and Robert, had moved away years before. Neither wanted to come back to live; they just wanted the money. Margaret had tried her best to raise enough money to purchase the land for a refuge, but the auction bid was three times more than she had to spend. Everyone knew an outsider had driven up the prices. All the locals wanted Margaret to have the property. None of them would bid against her. The thick and tangled woods were too difficult for the hunters to get through, but Margaret knew where there was a clearing to the water. Looking towards the water, she caught a glimpse at the waterfowl resting peacefully in their safe haven.

Margaret reached into the bag and handed John a biscuit. The two sat on a large log left after a tree had fallen. He reached in his pocket for a handkerchief for Margaret to wipe away the grease on her hand. Margaret shaded her eyes from the early morning sun and squinted at John. "I love Ms. Betty's link sausage biscuits, but you can see why I don't eat one every day."

A fleck of buttermilk biscuit clung to the tip of John's index finger from the lard Ms. Betty used in her biscuits. Turning, John flicked it in the opposite direction. "This biscuit can get kind of messy."

The two sat eating their food and listening to the sounds before trekking the rest of the way on foot. Margaret had a metal pail in her hand as she moved toward the birds. John watched her - she was lovely. A yearning stirred in him as the slender arm threw out the loose kernels to the waterfowl who fought hard for her attention. They screeched furiously, beating their wings and darting down to catch the easily accessible food that they didn't need to hunt for. Margaret turned to face him, and both tightly locked their eyes, fighting hard to resist each other.

Looking at her direction, John said, "It's beautiful here," John said. A gust of wind swooped in, fluttering the loose leaves. They stared toward the lake, Margaret walking to the edge to throw out the rest of the feed. John looked at her as she moved gracefully, putting more distance between them than he could stand.

John took in a deep breath, trying to control himself and slow his heartbeat. He didn't want to seem corny. Margaret could feel his eyes on her as she turned and stared in his direction. Repeating himself, John said, "This lake is so beautiful, I've never experienced so much natural beauty, Margaret."

Margaret laughed and nodded. "Yeah, I'm sure you just love the trees?"

"The trees are nice too," he answered as he grinned at her. She laughed under her breath, pleased, feeling his eyes on her. Trying to break his reverie, she asked, "What are you planning on doing with your law degree?"

Following her eyes as she stared across the lake, he said, "I don't know. Maybe work in the family law firm. It's a generational thing. What about you?"

She thought for a second, shaking her head. "I don't know. I'd like to travel the world, but I just couldn't stand to leave all this beauty." She looked at him seriously. "Most of all I just couldn't leave my dad. He's my best friend; we've been through so much together after my mother's death." She shrugged. "How about you John, any place you'd like to visit?"

He shook his head. "I don't know Margaret. I traveled a lot with my dad after my mother's death, but I've never felt a place as serene as Lake Mattamuskeet." Margaret smiled at John, their commonality of losing their mothers kept them both close to their dad's side.

Closing her eyes, Margaret took in a deep breath and held it for a moment. She began walking toward John. Before he realized it she was standing in front of him, both breathing hard and taking in the beauty around them. Margaret released her visual hold on him, taking the bucket to the truck for another load of feed.

Walking along the edge of the lake, the ground was soggy and covered with thick moss. John noticed a small row boat concealed with tree branches, possibly by the owner to either keep it from being seen or used by hunters.

Pulling back the branches, John inspected the small rowboat for rot and holes. The well-made teak wood showed no sign of wear or of lately being used. Looking further, John found paddles shoved under the seats. John had not rowed a boat since his college rowing days, but was ready to give it a try.

After hollering for Margaret; she grabbed the bucket of corn before getting in the small boat, John pushed it out into the lake before jumping in. He pulled on the paddles, allowing each stroke to glide the boat through the choppy waters.

Margaret had never seen this view from the lake. They floated like a decoy among the waterfowl, Margaret extending her arm out to softly touch the beautiful creatures, who displayed an affectionate acceptance to her as she fed them the feed. Margaret felt at home closely floating with all these beautiful birds.

Other than the wind moving the small boat, its main source of power had come to a stop. John stared with a sense of awe and wonder as he watched this magical moment between Margaret and the Tundra Swans. John watched as Margaret continued to feed the birds. The word must have gotten out; the boat was now surrounded by a wide range of waterfowl fighting for the kernels of corn. Margaret looked up at John, seeming overwhelmed by the sudden commotion of hungry birds. It was time to row towards a different direction.

"Look how the wind's picked up," Margaret said. The temperature seemed to have dropped twenty degrees in the last hour. Gusts of wind were now flowing in all directions, the lake's flat surface peaked with dancing waves. As the two sat staring, the clouds beyond began getting closer, dropping pellets of rain that quickly turned into freezing rain. The two watched the birds fleeing inside themselves, lowering their necks and pulling inward, retreating from the sudden climate change. Winds stirred the feathery balls bouncing up and down on the water.

John was paddling hard against the wind to shore. Grabbing Margaret's hand, he helped her out of the boat. They both pulled the boat further ashore, quickly throwing the branches back over the boat, they ran to the truck.

John and Margaret sat shivering in their damp clothes. John cranked up the truck, hoping the heater in the old truck wouldn't take long. Slowly the warm air could be felt. The rain had become a downpour of sleet that washed across the windshield faster than the wipers could work. The force of the downpour increased, becoming a continuous drumming on the hood of the truck.

Chapter 9

As they reached the farmhouse, Margaret got out while John put the truck in the barn. She ran inside to stoke the wood stove. As she turned around in the kitchen, she spied a note positioned upright to catch her attention. She knew her dad had already left early this morning for the farm meeting in Raleigh. His note reminded her to feed the cows tomorrow; he had already taken care of feeding them before he left.

Margaret whispered to herself, "Thank goodness." She jumped from the slamming of the door. Still startled, she looked up and noticed John standing in the doorway.

He laughed. "Are you okay?"

Grabbing the kettle, she filled it with water for coffee. "Yes, I was just reading the note my dad left. John, let me run and get you some dry clothes. I'll go check upstairs in dad's closet and see what I can find."

Margaret went upstairs to get some of Thomas's clothes, telling John to undress in the downstairs bathroom. When she came back downstairs, she softly knocked on the door. When it opened, John stood there with a towel wrapped around his waist, and for a second Margaret forgot she held the clothes in her arms until John reached out for them. Embarrassed by her awkward stare, she shoved the clothes into his hands and turned quickly towards the hissing sound in the kitchen. There, she poured the boiling water in the coffee cups, setting them on the kitchen table. Going out to the porch, the freezing rain stung her flushed face as she reached for the logs under the plastic cover. She pulled out two and brought them into the dry house, where the temperature was beginning to get cozy.

John walked into the kitchen as she held the cup of coffee up to her lips. A look of approval filled her eyes. She couldn't believe how good he looked in her father's clothes. They were a little big, but the rugged look was like one of the locals, even though the person inside had obviously been raised in a finer setting. Catching herself staring longer than she should, Margaret turned, pointing down to the filled coffee cup. Taking a big gulp, she told him, "John I brought some wood in to start a fire in the fireplace - see if you can get it started while I fix us dinner. There are matches on the mantle".

A few minutes later, she entered the living room with a tray of hot soup and roast beef sandwiches, leftovers from last night's dinner. Turning, he grinned, "I think the fire needs a little help."

Laying down the tray, Margaret reached for the poker. "Let me do it."

"Here, help yourself."

Margaret added a few sticks of kindling to the slow burning flame in the fireplace. Watching the wood catch fire, she glanced up at John, who stood holding a bowl of soup, staring at a painting heavily framed in gilt that looked out of place in the simplicity of the room.

Taking a spoonful of soup, he turned to look at Margaret and mumbled, "Huh, how did I miss this beautiful painting the other night?"

"It's my award-winning painting. I got the award when I was twelve." Margaret put her cup down on the coffee table and looked at it directly. "I gave the painting to my dad as a birthday gift. Lillian saw it and thought it should be entered in an art contest they were having at the Greenville Art School. It took first place over all the paintings entered."

John could see the woman in the painting resembled Margaret. The artist knew her subject, capturing the realism of even the smallest detail of the woman's beauty and gracefulness. John knew now where she had inherited her beauty. She turned, catching him looking at her. Staring back, Margaret thought how his brilliant blue eyes were so wide and honest. She smiled, and her eyes looked different now as she thought about her mother. The pain of her death was not completely gone, and she knew that it never would be.

"I still miss her. Sometimes I can still smell her scent when I sleep."

John reached out and touched her arm. "I'm sorry. I also lost my mother, when I was eight." He smiled at her, and she felt a warmer bond between them. John was easy to be with, so friendly, so warm. She wanted to touch his face, but she didn't dare.

Both reached for the same cup of coffee and laughed, when suddenly the lights blinked off, leaving only the red embers of the fire glowing brightly. Margaret found her way to the kitchen, reaching above the cabinet for the oil lamp. She lit it with a match and took it into the living room, where John put another log in the fireplace. The crackling wood made the shadows cast by the flames dance around the room.

The evening passed as both Margaret and John sat captured by the warmth in the room. Margaret got up to turn the oil lamp's flame down lower. The flames from the fireplace were hypnotic, and soon Margaret fell asleep in the comfort of John's arms.

Looking down at Margaret, John thought how strongly he felt about her. Something was happening; he was falling in love, but this time it was different. His connection to Margaret seemed real; she connected to life like no other woman he had ever met, constantly appreciating and protecting everything that surrounded her.

John had been in love once with a girl he had met at Harvard. There were very few women at the college, but the ones he knew were independent and smart. Catherine was not only smart, but also beautiful. She came from an aristocratic family from Yorkshire, England, and it was obvious when she spoke. John had been caught off guard when they met. Catherine had joined a study group he had been a part of since starting law school; they all tried to study but most of them, including Catherine, would usually end up at a local bar afterwards. John and Catherine would go off together, making the most of the evening by spending the night together at Catherine's townhouse. They had been inseparable until their last semester of law school. Catherine had begun drifting away from him, making excuses about needing to get more serious about school, and so they stopped seeing each other. A month before graduation, John saw Catherine with another classmate huddled together in a booth, their lips locked tightly. Neither saw him as he passed by their table.

John never saw Catherine again. He had been glad school was ending and ready to get back home to start practicing law in the family firm, but then his best friend Nathanial Webber proposed they take off a year and travel, saying they would have plenty of time to get serious about life. Now, he owed his good fortune to his friend as he lay beside the most beautiful woman he'd ever seen. Her simplistic life appealed more to him than what he had ever experienced with Catherine. The beating sound of the ice pellets hitting the tin roof eased John's tired thoughts.

Grabbing the heavy wool blanket, he covered himself and Margaret.

Hearing the distant sound of a tractor, John looked over his shoulder to find Margaret curled up against his back. Her body was contoured to the shape of his, forming a single solid shape under the covers, much like two matching pieces of a puzzle. The chilling temperature outside of the covers told John that the fire was almost burned out, making him relish her body's warmth and fragrant smell. He watched the morning trickle through the drapes and lighten the night shadows in the room.

John came from a family of privilege, with servants who kept the family warm and fed. Each family member had a private servant who did everything for that person, making sure the proper clothing was laid out for any occasion and even helping them dress, or running their bath water and making sure it was to their liking. The help laid out their night clothes across the bed linens, and even turned the covers down at bedtime. John liked Ms. Melba, she had been with him since he was a baby, always complaining how he wouldn't let her do her job. John was probably the most self-sufficient one in the family. His brother William was still too young to take care of himself, their dad, Howard, left early and worked late at the law firm, and his mother Mary had suffered a stroke while giving birth to William and was bedridden before passing away five years later.

Looking at the simplicity of the farm, he couldn't help but think how the Windleys had created this life for themselves through hard work. This self-sufficient way of living made you appreciate a fire burning in the wood stove, but when it was cold you'd better get it started or you would freeze to death.

John shivered as his sock feet touched the cold floor. He quietly tiptoed to where he had left his shoes, quickly slipping them on before stepping out to grab a couple of logs for the stove. As he opened the door he saw a ruddy-faced man standing there who looked shocked to see John.

Before John could say anything, the man quickly asked where Margaret was. The concern in his voice caught John's attention. Paul Rogers was a hardy man who liked to take charge of things and who protected everyone around him. Stumbling over his words, John quickly introduced himself.

Although he hesitated before grabbing John's hand, Paul Rogers suddenly began to smile as though he remembered something. "Well young man, it's a pleasure to meet you. Thomas told me all about you." Paul continued to stare with his hazel eyes, shifting his stance. His swaying shoulders and rough hands showed wear from years of hard farm labor. Feeling a little uncomfortable, John didn't know what to say.

Paul began to laugh, "It's okay John. It seems Thomas knew you might be hanging out here while he was in Raleigh."

John felt awkward, and his already chilled face completely froze at Paul's remark.

Paul let out a robust laugh saying, "Don't worry, if Thomas didn't like you he would have told me to bring my shotgun when I came over to check on Margaret."

Now, that broke the tension and John began laughing. "Mr. Rogers, I learned a few days back that Margaret can stand her own ground; I have a lot of respect for her and Mr. Windley."

Paul, realizing Thomas was right about John, smiled and told John to let Margaret know he would feed the cows.

Letting out a cold sigh, John reached with his frozen hands to pick up the logs. Opening the iron door, he could see the scattered red embers. When he put the dry wood inside it quickly ignited into a roaring fire, heating up the cold room. John hadn't expected to feel so proud over something he had always taken for granted. He stood back smiling at his accomplishment.

After pouring water into the metal tea kettle he set it on the wood stove. The fire heated up the cold water and its spout spewed an occasional cloud of steam until it reached its boiling point. When it pushed out a continuous flow of water vapors, John lifted the kettle off of the stove and poured the boiling water into the coffee cups. A hissing sound accompanied the slosh of the hot water poured into the cold cups.

Margaret rolled onto her back. The sunlight beaming from the window into the room lit up her face. John set the coffee cups on the table and quietly sat down. He softly pushed the hair away from Margaret's face as she slept. She stirred, finally opening her eyes to smile at him.

He whispered, "You look like a sleeping princess."

Sitting up, she reached for the cup, she inched over to him, pulling the covers over their laps. Through the window she could hear the sound of a tractor in the distance, probably Paul taking feed to his cows. John stared at her wondering eyes, waiting patiently for her to return to him from a night of sleep.

Rubbing her eyes, Margaret whispered, "Thanks for getting the fire started. I hope it wasn't too hard."

John looked over at her, smiling. "Not too bad."

Smiling back, she whispered, "How does it look outside? I've got to feed the cows."

John turned and looked out the window. "Mr. Rogers is going to feed the cows."

Margaret gasped. "What do you mean?"

Turning back, John gently touched her face, telling Margaret about Paul stopping to check on her, and at first how intimidated he had made John feel. They both laughed.

Looking out, Margaret could see the ice had crystallized and that the sun's rays were making everything sparkle.

Chapter 10

The cold hours of the early morning besieged Lillian as she took off her coat and laid it carefully on the chair. She turned the radio on low. The pendulum of the cuckoo clock ticked softly, swinging above the brown wooden table. In the distance she could hear the sound of a tractor stirring the soil. Looking across the field, she could see that the edges still showed signs of yesterday's ice storm. Staring further, she could see lights burning at the Windley farmhouse. Paul was going to stop in to check on Margaret before he fed the cows.

Grabbing the eggs from each pocket of her dress, she gently placed them in the basket. She reached for the yellow cotton smock hanging on the hook. Its gay color brightened her salt-and-pepper hair, cut short enough to be pin curled for body. Lillian's compassionate blue eyes gave anyone who met her a sense of comfort that made them feel special. The room had a view of the two story barn built for the farm equipment. It stood nearby, weathered from years of exposure to the elements. Its gray washed-out appearance made the already gloomy day feel colder.

Caught up in her thoughts, Lillian mindlessly turned the water on to wash the dishes. As she hunched over the sink, she was unaware that Margaret had come in and was standing in the room. As she turned, for a second she was startled. She put the cast iron pan back into the greasy water and grabbed the towel to dry her wet soapy hands before hugging Margaret.

"Oh, Margaret! I was just thinking about you!" Smiling, she looked out the window. "Did Paul stop by this morning?"

Margaret nodded her head. "He did Lil."

Smiling, Lillian squeezed Margaret's hand, saying, "Well I'm glad he did! With that nasty ice storm yesterday, I was worried about you staying there alone without Thomas. Are you hungry?"

Shaking her head, Margaret answered, "No Lil, I had a muffin earlier, how about just coffee." She took the cup Lillian handed her, adding cream and sugar.

Lillian turned to finish washing the pan. She took a moment to look at Margaret as she sat down. Her usual fresh complexion seemed flushed and overcast with a distant look of silence. Lillian leaned herself against the sink, drying her hands as she contemplated Margaret. She laid her hand lightly on Margaret's arm, applying a faint pressure.

Margaret stared at Lillian, trying to think of something to say. "Have you been to the Lodge lately, Lil?" she asked.

"Not lately." She was very brief. "What is going on Margaret?"

Margaret didn't answer right away. Instead she got up, looking out at the drooping greenness above the frozen ground. She flopped back down in the chair and tried to empty her mouth, fumbling over words, but becoming more coherent as Lillian continued to listen with kindness in her eyes. She looked at Lillian with an expression of anguish.

"I'm in love," she said softly.

Lillian began to smile and then stopped herself, seeing the confused look in Margaret's eyes. "But that's wonderful, Margaret. Who's the lucky guy?" She was surprised to hear Margaret talk about being in love with one of the hunters, but didn't let it show. However, her surprise at the name of the man made Lillian make an odd, sharp gesture. The curious cast in her eyes turned inward.

She spoke in a tone of incredulity. "Who? John Ashton!" The words caught in her throat and changed to a low complex moan. Lillian intently stared at Margaret, who stared back with embarrassment.

Margaret got up, laughing as she clutched the back of the chair. "Yes Lil, John Ashton."

Her words dug deep, Lillian's eyes sharply staring in disbelief. "My God Margaret, are you for real?"

Smiling, Margaret shook her head up and down. "Yes, Lil! John and I have been spending a lot of time together. I have never met anyone who makes me feel like John does. Lil, I know without a doubt I am in love."

Lillian's cynicism gave way to happiness, and she jumped up to throw her arms around the only person who was like a daughter to her. "Okay, well when can Paul and I meet him?"

Margaret tightly hugged Lillian, then stood back, excited to say, "Paul's already met him."

Scanning Margaret's face, Lillian said, "He has? Paul didn't say anything to me about meeting John."

Margaret hesitated before explaining her last couple of days with John. She was worried Lillian would be upset with her. "John just left for the Lodge to help Davenport with some legal matters, but you can meet him this weekend at the annual Christmas celebration."

Lillian knew Paul never wanted to worry her with anything; he knew how protective she was of Margaret. Lillian smiled and gave her a hug. "Well I cannot wait to meet him, Margaret."

Margaret knew it was time to get to the lake. "Lil, I've got to go, but I need a dress. I need to spend all day tomorrow finishing the paintings for Saturday, so the only day I have to get one is Thursday. Let's drive to Greenville!"

Lillian smiled. "I'll be ready at 9:00 a.m."

On, Thursday Margaret got up early and crossed the hall to the room her dad had designated as Margaret's art studio. The large room stretched east and west, and its windows captured a view of the sunrises and sunsets - the perfect lighting for an artist. Margaret sat on the stool with the flat of her hand pressed against the side of her face and stared at her easel. Its backside faced the door; she didn't like anyone standing behind her as she painted or seeing any of her unfinished art work. Two other easels draped with white sheets stood around the room - paintings to be sent to the Lodge before hunting season was over. This was the time of year Margaret sold most of her paintings. On Wednesday, she spent all day in the tree stand painting; only taking a break when John stopped by with a picnic lunch prepared by the Lodge staff. He promised he would not stay long, but after lunch, he stayed to explore the area while she painted; they couldn't resist being without each other.

Uncovering the painting, Margaret smiled. The brush strokes gently filled in his masculine features; the wide angular jaw, square chin and prominent brow made her shudder with excitement. Every moment spent with John, she saw something different about him but she wasn't going to get the time to finish the painting. As she pulled the sheet back over the canvas she glanced at the clock. She knew Lillian was ready for their trip to Greenville. Looking out of the windows, Margaret could see that the countryside had begun to thaw, which would make it easier to plow the fields.

Margaret slowed the truck just before the straight line of trees deeply burrowed along the edge of the Jessup Farm. For a second they blocked her view, and then she saw Henry standing at the edge of the field watching her as she drove past. Lillian smiled and waved at Henry from the passenger seat. Margaret still hesitated from embarrassment, though she told herself she was being silly.

As they slowly passed she waved, but he didn't wave back. She told herself it was because Henry was busy getting ready to plow the field. She watched him in her rear view mirror as he stepped onto the tractor and sat down on the tractor seat, clenching the steering wheel. Henry still stared in her direction, and she thought how they had always spoken to each other, until John had come into her life. Now they rarely saw each other anymore. Margaret kept driving, smiling softly at Lillian, who seemed to know what she was thinking.

Both women silently looked ahead at the winding road. Margaret nudged the gas pedal with her foot, the steering wheel warm from her hands. Her thoughts now were of John, making her insides jump. She smiled to herself.

"What time is Thomas coming home?" Lillian asked.

Margaret had almost forgotten about her dad arriving from Raleigh today. Her stomach tightened at how he would react to her feelings about John. She said, "Around 4 p.m. I forgot to leave him a note! I guess I was distracted."

Lillian laughed at Margaret's thoughtlessness. She knew what the distraction was. "I'm sure Thomas will stop by the house to see Paul before going home."

Shortly after eleven they arrived in Greenville. They drove slowly down Main Street, looking at the store fronts. Margaret caught a glimpse of a young woman pushing a stroller who looked about her own age. Margaret hadn't thought about being a mother. She felt there was a lot more to do before having such a big responsibility.

Lillian pointed at one of the store fronts. "There it is: Sylvia's Dress and Gown Boutique."

Margaret quickly pulled in to park in front of the store. The two walked inside, and were immediately ambushed by a well put together woman whose red smile seemed to be drawn on her white porcelain face. Aerosol kept every strand of her hair in place. Margaret knew what she wanted. The sales lady brought out three dresses she thought would work, but the last dress was it. The emerald green dress had satin cupped sleeves and sheer fabric covering the arms, which were attached to a square neckline with tiny sequins delicately sewn with silk thread. The narrow sash enhanced her tiny waist.

Margaret had never tried on anything so elegant - she bought most of her clothes at Gibbs Store. If she couldn't find something there, Mr. Gibbs would order what she needed. After slipping on the heels, she stepped out of the dressing room. Her beauty snatched every set of eyes in the store. She thought the sales woman's face would crack when she smiled with approval, gesturing for Margaret to turn around.

As she watched her spin, the saleswoman whispered, "The perfect figure, beautiful."

Lillian sniveled at the sight as Margaret faced her, shaking her head back and forth. Her outstretched arms wrapped around Margaret. Staring in the mirror, Lillian noticed the length was too long, and realized they didn't have three days to wait for the store's seamstress to hem the dress. She'd do it herself Friday morning.

Margaret begged for Lillian to pick herself out a dress, but Lillian said she would make her own. However, as they walked through the store Margaret noticed Lillian kept her eye on one dress in particular, an elegant black satin dress with a lacy high neckline. Margaret encouraged Lillian to try on the dress. As she walked out of the dressing room, Lillian looked exquisite, like Margaret had never seen her look before. Farm life kept both women isolated from any elegance, but the annual Lodge Christmas Ball gave everyone the opportunity to show off their store-bought finery.

As Lillian went to take off the perfectly fitted dress, Margaret turned to smile at the saleswoman. "I'll take both these dresses."

Lillian came out of the dressing room in time to hear. She waved her right hand at the saleslady saying, "No"! Turning back to Margaret, Lillian adamantly said, "Margaret, I've got my dress."

Margaret resisted Lillian's offer saying, "Lil, I've done very well selling my paintings. Let's just say its partial payment for all those art lessons you gave me as a child." Lil, just kept mumbling to herself.

Ignoring her, Margaret kept talking to the sales lady. "I've got to do some more shopping. Let me pay you for them, and we will be back in a couple of hours to pick them up."

As she stared at the woman, Margaret noticed that she had a single strand of hair out of place, which caught the yellow rays of the sun streaming through the large window. Margaret thought how over time, staying in one place too long could cause a person to begin to mimic their environment. She thought about how her attire fit the life surrounding Lake Mattamuskeet, and wondered what people would think when they saw her Saturday night at the Christmas Ball dressed like a store mannequin.

Chapter 11

Thomas returned home from Raleigh on Thursday. His return was delayed by the ice storm, and the drive back was long and mentally consuming. Each mile seemed to drag out longer than normal. Thomas arrived in the afternoon hours, stopping at Gibbs Store when he saw Paul's truck parked outside. The store was packed with locals trying to get that special outfit for Saturday night's Christmas Ball at the Lodge. Paul stood around with the men who waited for their wives. He let Thomas know Lillian and Margaret had gone to Greenville. With all the commotion in the room, Paul forgot to mention anything to Thomas about seeing John at the house. The men anxiously waited for the details of Thomas' meeting in Raleigh; Thomas assured everyone they could continue using the lake to irrigate their fields during the drought months. The news brought the excitement of Christmas and the success of another year of farming.

That night, Thomas reminded Margaret he was spending the majority of the day working at the Lodge to help Lawrence prepare for Saturday night's party. Margaret assured her dad she would be joining him as soon as Lillian finished hemming her dress. She hugged her dad before going to bed. As she eased up the stairs, she wondered why her dad never mentioned anything about John coming over while he was in Raleigh. Apparently Paul must had forgotten, or he was too tired to talk about it.

Margaret got started early the following morning - it was the day before the Christmas Ball and she needed to finish a couple of paintings before going over to the Roger's. As she got out of bed, her thoughts gave way to anxiety at the thought of John leaving for New York on Sunday.

Grabbing her robe, she quietly tiptoed to her art studio to finish the paintings for sale on Saturday during the Christmas Ball. The dawn's rays began to break in such a way they split apart, giving rise to the sun. Its warmth beamed across the field, giving a natural light to the room. Margaret sat before this stillness for a moment and thanked God for the serenity. Opening her eyes, something across the room caught her attention. Walking to the other end of the room, Margaret uncovered the painting. She stared at his face; every stroke of the brush captured the man's likeness, except for his eyes. For days the white eye sockets had stared back at her, waiting for her to complete the blank stare. She tried to find the right image in her memories of him to paint them, but her mind would not let the paint brush in her hand capture the essence of the person she had fallen in love with. Instead, she opted to finish the other paintings before heading over to Lillian's.

Margaret stood patiently on the stool while Lillian knelt and carefully added some pins to the hem of her gown. Taking another pin from between her lips, Lillian mumbled something that sounded like, "This is a good color for your complexion, especially your eyes." After taking the final pin from between her lips, her words became coherent: "There, that should do it. Now walk around the room so I can see how it moves."

With pins embellishing the hem of the dress, Margaret danced around the room, pulling Lillian up off the floor. The two twirled around, feeling dizzy, and fell across the bed, giggling.

Staring at Margaret for a second, trying to catch her breath, Lillian pushed Margaret's hair away from her face. "I could never have children Margaret, but you will always be like a daughter to me."

Tears welled up in Margaret's eyes. Reaching for Lillian, she gave her a big hug, softly speaking. "Lil, you made me who I am, you have taught me everything about painting, which has allowed me to put the beauty around here on canvas. It would be an honor to have you as my mother." Tears streamed down both their faces as each gave the other a hug.

As she climbed out of the truck at the Lodge, Margaret saw a group of men circled around and hollering. Someone was fighting in the human rink. Each time a fist struck it aroused the crowd into a loud frenzy. For several seconds all she could hear was a clamor of voices until Elbert, a friend of Henry, shouted, "Henry watch out, John's getting back up." Margaret quickly ran towards the group of men, elbowing herself through the crowd. Making her way through the tight bond, Margaret caught a glimpse of John on the ground looking around groggily. Margaret gasped at the sight of his bloody face. She wanted to run over to John, but felt herself being restrained by a pair of hands. Trying to kick herself from the hold, Margaret screamed his name. "Henry! Henry! Stop it!"

Henry never acknowledged Margaret's request. Henry's strike to the jaw had John reaching for the pain and making a face, flinching. Sighing deeply from the touch, he slowly got to his feet. He stood staring at Henry with fire in his eyes. Henry began to laugh at John, gloating at his victory. John had gained his composure and stood solid, his usually sunny disposition darkened suddenly to anger.

John lunged forward and struck Henry with a closed fist. Henry's laughter died to a short, hoarse gasp. The sound of the jeering men became a hollow, echoing noise in his ears. Henry staggered drunkenly, losing consciousness. His face drained of color and his mouth went slack, silencing his taunting words.

"Stop it!" It was useless; Margaret was beginning to get impatient with them. She broke from her restraints. The tight circle of men were still yelling, "Fight! Fight!"

Margaret grabbed John's arm, pulling him away from the mob of men. Most were Henry's friends, and were now yelling wildly for Henry to "Get up," whooping and hollering encouragements to continue fighting.

John felt Margaret's voice calming him. His body rigid, the muscles in his jaw working, he stared down at Henry. Taking a deep breath, he allowed Margaret to drag him away from the commotion.

John and Margaret hesitated as Thomas and Lawrence came running out, shouting for the men to break it up and get back to work. Thomas went down to check on Henry, who, not wanting to look like a loser, was trying to get up on his feet. Standing on the sidelines, John was still fuming. Head up, eyes cast heavenward, hands clasped behind his back, he walked briskly back and forth, trying to calm himself. Margaret was furious with Henry and his friends, who continued to call taunting words towards her and John.

Thomas took Henry into the Lodge to bandage him up, scolding him for starting the fight. Margaret sat John down on the stoop. She caressed his shoulders, then squatted in front of him. Reaching up, she held his face between her hands, her eyes imploring him frantically. "John, I'm sorry."

Agitation still burned in his eyes, but the alluring sound of her voice captured his attention with the words, "I love you."

Chapter 12

Never had Margaret Windley appeared more lady-like than in the long, flowing green gown made of silk. Cut perfectly, it outlined her body in all the right places. Those who knew her had expected something less than this rich beauty. From the look on her brightly smiling face, which seemingly expressed the attitude of her spirit, those who knew her began to guess that Margaret Windley was in love. John Ashton stood beside her in a finely-cut suit, his dark curly brown hair and striking blue eyes conjuring an impression of wealth and achievement. Both complimented each other. Holding tightly to her hand, John Windley led Margaret inside the beautifully decorated room.

The moment that solidified everyone's belief came a few minutes later, when John led Margaret out onto the dance floor. They both embraced, holding onto each other as though someone were trying to rip them apart. His arms wrapped around her svelte figure, evident in the clinging gown.

"You're the prettiest girl here, Margaret." His voice was soft in her ear, and his arms felt powerful around her. She blushed, tossing her hair off her shoulders. John danced her around the floor so he could show her off, and it was easy to see why he was so proud of her.

As they bumped up against his best friend Nathanial, who was dancing with one of the locals, John winked at him. Nathanial, who had driven the two of them down from

New York and would soon drive John back, knew it was going to be hard separating the two. As they twirled past, Nathanial smiled at Margaret; he thought instantly that she was the most spectacularly beautiful woman he had ever seen.

John held Margaret tight, and his lips gently brushed the top of her head. After he danced her over to a corner, he tilted her chin up with one hand so he could look directly into those exquisite emerald eyes again. "I'll miss you."

Teary eyed, Margaret felt her heart ache, but before she could react she felt herself being twirled around like a ballerina, her honey-colored hair flying loose around her face. In reality, both knew this was their last night together. John Ashton was leaving the next morning for New York City, but he promised to return to his beloved Margaret whenever he settled his affairs with his father, Howard. He loved Margaret, who looked more beautiful than any person in the room had ever seen her.

Staring at John, it was as though she had tunnel vision. She knew all eyes were on them, but all Margaret saw were the piercing blue eyes staring back at her. Reaching up, she softly touched his bruised cheek.

He was falling for her, and she for him. She turned to face him, and he kissed her, and she kissed him back. As the band played, the two freely danced around the room. Everyone stood watching the two connected bodies swaying to the slow beat of the music, both locked together tightly, as if hoping Father Time would allow them to have this moment forever.

Closing her eyes, Margaret rested her head on John's chest as he carried her around the room. Suddenly, the beat began to pick up. Everyone standing around began dancing, laughing together as the Christmas Spirit filled the room. The heavily decorated room was crowded with locals and visitors who felt excited as they watched Lawrence take the mic from the band director, with laughter in the air, the auction began.

The donated items went fast. Then, Lawrence called out for Margaret to step forward to explain her "prize" painting. Still feeling John's kiss on her lips, she stepped on stage with enthusiasm. Thomas followed her to the podium, where he anxiously stood-by listening. Margaret graciously thanked everyone for their applause, then she began her introduction to the covered painting.

As she told the story tears gathered in her eyes. As she described each feathery creature in the painting, she stared out into a crowd who stared back in disbelief at how something so rare could happen in such a small community. When she removed the blue cloth a loud gasp echoed throughout the room. The short audible intake of breath faded away as everyone in the room stood in a state of enchantment. Each could not believe their eyes - how does someone capture such realism by using a mixture of paints on a canvas?

Lawrence's call for bids released the enchantment in the room. Many of the Lodge's resident hunters stood in front of the stage clamoring for a chance to bid. The locals were forced to step back, each knowing they could not compete with such wealth. The locals were grateful for all the money the "outsiders" spent in their community. Many of them benefited from all this wealth.

The bidding surpassed everyone's imagination. Each bid was repeated by the lively emotions of the locals - the outrageous dollar amounts made it difficult for them to contain their excitement. They rarely experienced such wealth being thrown out. Many had worked months farming their crops, hoping for a fraction of the bidding amounts. The full moon shone brightly through the windows, encompassing the room and making the night feel even more exciting.

John looked down at Margaret and softly whispered, "I've got something I want you to see." Reaching for her hand, he carried her through the crowd, which was too distracted to know they had even left the room. Running up to the second floor, the two hurried towards the tower door. After grabbing one of the lanterns used by the hunters, they opened the door and both climbed the 121 iron steps of the spiraling staircase to the observatory at the top of the tower. With their adrenaline flowing, both did not feel the fatigue most felt after making the climb.

Looking out of the observatory, the moon illuminated everything around. John pointed out to a cove where the white disk spotlighted each feathery bird tucked inside the crevices along the waters' edge. The view made Margaret wish she had a canvas before her. She composed the painting she would make of the scene in her head, already trying to memorialize the rare opportunity to witness this spectacular view with the one person whom she had fallen in love.

Margaret and John held each other as they looked out, knowing this moment wouldn't last long. The two passionately kissed. They wanted to spend every second left with the other, instead of returning to the party. They both ran towards John's room, needing privacy to give them time alone to share their last night together before John left for New York.

John smiled at Margaret. All they wanted was for this moment to last. As she looked up into his eyes Margaret could feel his warmth. John lifted her chin to kiss her full lips. She felt herself physically being pulled toward him, she wanted him.

When the moment seemed right, the beautiful gown fell in a heap of green organza. The flesh color slip clung to her perfect frame. He didn't want to overpower her. Not now, not the first time. Staring into her eyes, John asked, "Would you rather wait?"

Margaret was too caught up in the moment to wait. Being in his arms, she felt as though she were almost floating. As she stepped out of the gown that clung to her ankles she suddenly felt his hands on her breasts. Desire exploding in her head as he shed his clothes. She felt herself drift away in his powerful arms. She didn't want to wait at all.

John parted her legs and touched her body with his lips.

Margaret felt tears of joy streaming down her face as pleasure exploded between her legs. John looked into Margaret's eyes as the tears streamed down her face, gently kissing her, whispering how much he loved her. Wrapping his arms around her, he tucked her body next to him, holding her tight. John never wanted to let her go, but both knew the inevitable would eventually happen as the moment lingered into the early morning.

Margaret awoke as the morning sun lit up her face. Staring at their two naked bodies, their legs wrapped around each other, Margaret thought how perfect they were for one another. She could smell the sweetness coming from John's body, the same cologne he'd worn the night he came for dinner. Not wanting this moment to end, she tried hard to wash away the thoughts of her father sitting at the kitchen table worrying about where she was. Margaret whispered to John, "I need to get home before my dad worries about me."

John came to life, raising up his arm and rolling on his side to face Margaret. For a second she studied his muscular build, thinking how gently he had made love to her. Reaching up, she brushed his hair away from his face. As he slowly woke up, he stared straight into her eyes, mumbling to her, "I love you."

Margaret didn't know whether to laugh or cry. It wasn't the right time for this; she wanted him to stay longer than an hour. John hadn't expected what he saw as he stared into her eyes, tears overflowing onto the sheets, Margaret didn't want him to leave.

Trying to form the words, Margaret told him, "John, I love you too, I just didn't want this day to end so quickly. I feel we've just gotten to really know one another, and it's just not fair."

John smiled at her argument. He knew it wasn't fair to leave Margaret so soon. Pulling her closer to him, he felt the moment was becoming more than he could stand. He cupped her face in his hands and desperately kissed her lips. Both couldn't resist softly moaning as they clung tightly to each other's body.

Cleaning the three hour sleep from their eyes, they both clothed themselves. They slipped out of the back door, not wanting anyone to see them. Luckily last night's party had kept most of the still intoxicated occupants in their bed, and the hunters couldn't hunt on Sunday, so most slept late.

As the two stepped outside, they noticed Lawrence stood smiling on the back porch. He tossed the truck key in John's direction. Embarrassed, Margaret didn't say anything as she slipped in the passenger seat. John thanked Lawrence before opening the driver's door.

Before they drove off, Lawrence let Margaret know her painting had been bought for $1,000.00 by someone who wanted to stay anonymous. Margaret was still blushing from the embarrassing moment, but gasped when she heard the amount. John reached for her hand to congratulate her.

As John drove her home, Margaret was silent, looking out the window at the storm clouds beginning to gather in the distance. As they turned toward her house, Margaret balled her fists into her gown with nervousness. She knew her dad would be awake, and anxiously waiting for her arrival home.

John stopped the truck far away from the farmhouse, hoping Thomas would not hear the noisy engine. They sat looking at each other for a long time, each with a lot to say, but no way to say it.

Staring at Margaret, John thought he had never seen a more beautiful face, even though there was sorrow and pain and anguish staring back at him. Finally John grabbed her hands. Removing her gloves, he rubbed the soft delicate hands and then held them to his lips and kissed them. Tears flowed as Margaret tried to talk. And then, without even wanting to say the words, Margaret quietly said, "I'll miss you John."

John sat staring at her eyes, which were pleading with him not to leave. John said, "I'm sorry to leave you so quickly, but I promise to return as quickly as I leave you." And suddenly the tears he had fought back sprang into his eyes, and he started to turn away. Margaret grabbed his arm and pulled him back. He looked down at her, and gently smoothed a hand over her silky hair. John felt he couldn't take his hands or lips from her again; neither wanted to let go. It was almost painful when at last she tore herself away.

Tears flowed as Margaret began the journey towards the house, the long green gown dragging, its edges sweeping away anything in its path. As she reached the front door, she reluctantly turned to wave good-by, but was startled to see John coming up the steps with a look of desperation in his eyes. He reached out and grabbed her before she stepped inside, and the two embraced each other for the last time. John repeatedly told her he loved her, and she repeated the same words.

As John drove away from the farmhouse, he could see her standing on the porch waving. Putting up his hand, he waved back, rolling down the window and shouting, "I'll see you in two weeks." As he stopped at the end of the drive, he could still faintly see her on the porch. Standing in the doorway for the last instant, Margaret waved at him, and then the green gown disappeared from his life.

John had never met a woman who energized his soul like Margaret. He loved her simplicity, he loved the clarity of her dreams, but most of all he love the power she had to paint the beauty around her. Her bravery in expressing how she felt about the hunters who killed the birds she painted, her sharp opinions, her stormy moods and sudden, deep laughter unfolded within him, creating a new level of attraction he could not resist, but this turbulence in him was torture, knowing he would be leaving her in two hours to return to New York. John knew it would be difficult leaving, but he promised himself, as he had promised Margaret, that he would return after he took the law exam and settled his affairs with his dad.

John knew his dad would forbid him to leave New York City; he expected John to take his place at the law firm where three generations of Ashtons had practiced law. Yet John couldn't wait to return to her.

Chapter 13

John Ashton left for New York on a day scoured by a slow drizzling rain. It was a few days before Christmas. Margaret lay in bed with the covers pulled to her neck, wanting to cocoon herself in the comfort of her bed until John returned, afraid to lose his scent from her body, his words from her thoughts. Staring at nothing in particular, her mind wandered to the last night's events. The one moment that stayed in her mind was him staring into her eyes. Margaret felt sure that he would return quickly, as soon as he could.

At the closing of New Year's Eve, Margaret sat at the large bay window of the Lodge, wondering what John was doing tonight. The year was coming to a close and the clock was about to strike midnight. Looking around the room, she could see Henry standing in the corner with Rebecca Frazier. He had one arm around her and the other propped up against the wall, both physically ready for the clock to signal the New Year. It almost hurt to look at the two caught up in such a romantic pose.

Henry was a passionate man with a wild and moody side. Margaret knew how to tame his short-temper, but not many women could handle him as she could. As if he sensed her staring at him, he turned and smiled at her, and their eyes met and held the way two people suddenly recognize one another across the room. Henry nodded. Margaret smiled gratefully, then looked into the flames, thinking about how someone else seemed to have finally caught his heart.

Margaret glanced across the room and a smile flicked on her lips. She turned to the painting of the paired Tundra Swans, the same picture John had told her he loved. She remembered her reaction when he had told her how much he loved the painting, how she had been short and condescending towards him, yet throughout he had still kept his sweetness and sincerity. It brought tears to her eyes as she thought of it, and she turned her face away from everyone's view.

Lillian watched Margaret staring up at the wall, wondering what she was thinking. Although everyone knew who Margaret was thinking about, no one really knew what to say to her. John should have arrived yesterday; he'd told Lawrence he would return to the Lodge to help decorate for the New Year celebration.

Lillian reached out for two glasses of champagne. She walked over to Margaret, setting them on the table. "Hey sweetheart, a penny for your thoughts."

Margaret tried hard to keep her composure. When her tears welled up to the point of overflowing, she turned her head and wiped them away with her sleeve. Lil stroked her hair with one hand while holding Margaret's hand with the other. Getting up, Margaret apologized to Lillian and immediately walked out of the room towards the bathroom.

Lawrence stood in the hall. "You okay Margaret?" he asked as she passed.

Before she could answer, the tears poured out, leaving Lawrence speechless. He grabbed her hand and reached inside his pocket to pull out a key, whispering "number eight."

Margaret, looking puzzled, took the key and headed up the stairs towards the end of the hall. There she stood, listening to the clock strike one, two, three, four... At the strike of five she was inside the room. Looking around, she recognized John's belongings. Margaret realized he had left almost everything, including the shotguns he had never used again after their first encounter. As the clock struck twelve, she laid across the bed, now once again sure that John would be returning to her; he had probably gotten delayed by the winter storm blowing through the northeast.

Margaret grabbed the pillow and inhaled deeply. She was barely able to smell him. Hugging it tighter, she began sobbing.

Margaret knew she was being petty, and she felt horrible about ignoring Henry's calls, but she was still fuming over his treatment of John, and she knew he would just say something disparaging about John and make her angry again – that he was spoiled and rich with no desire to ever return to Lake Mattamuskeet.

Margaret turned the television off and looked up to see her dad asleep in his recliner; she wondered at what point he had lost interest. Maybe he had already heard this same small talk about Henry too many times, and had grown bored from the repetitious conversation.

Margaret bent down to softly whisper in her dad's ear, "Hey dad, it's late, I'm going up to bed." As usual, Thomas mumbled something about being up in a second. Margaret knew the routine on Sunday nights; Thomas always slept in the recliner until dawn. The supine position seemed to elevate his legs enough to keep them from cramping, allowing him to get a good night's sleep.

Months had passed since she last saw John, and the morning sickness had just begun to subside. Now only an occasional smell made her nauseous. She tried hard to hide her condition from everyone, especially her dad, but sometimes he stared at her with suspicion. Margaret felt her condition would upset the people closest to her, making her keep the secret tight within the realm of herself. Margaret didn't know who to trust. She wanted so badly to tell Lillian, but knew she could not bear to see disappointment in her face. Margaret wore most of her shirts outside the waist of her pants and layered it with a jacket. She hardly went anywhere, especially not to the Lodge. Margaret didn't want to be inundated with questions about John.

The next afternoon, Henry called again, asking her to lunch at Ms. Betty's. His sweet demeanor caught her off guard. Speaking before thinking, Margaret gave into the feeling of loneliness and longing, and agreed to see her friend.

Chapter 14

Margaret and Henry sat at a table in Ms. Betty's cafe, both sipping iced tea. Margaret knew that she and Henry's bond was inseparable, despite how angry he might have been making her lately. He never wavered in his love for her, despite anything she put him through. At times Margaret wasn't completely aware of his love; she was too involved in her memories of John and reluctant to listen to the voice in her head that was telling her she was wasting her time.

Henry said, "Remember New Year's Eve?"

Margaret nodded, "Yeah, I remember."

He laughed. "How the two of us couldn't keep our eyes off each other?"

Margaret smiled. "No, your eyes were on me," she said, "I was thinking about John." She hesitated, realizing what she had just said. Her cheeks lit up with embarrassment. "I'm so sorry Henry, I'm just being foolish. Please, forgive me."

Henry shrugged, "Forgiven." He let out a sigh. "I understand Margaret, I really do." As Henry spoke, he began to feel uncomfortable, and his voice seemed to lose its stride. "I'd like to apologize for saying all those bad things about John." He was slouched forward towards Margaret, as though someone could hear his conversation. Since it was 3:00 p.m., the slowest time of the day, other than Ms. Betty and the waitress, they were the only customers.

103

Margaret cleared her throat. Apparently her expression seemed to alarm Henry, causing him to suddenly sit back in the booth and intently stare at her. Margaret saw that he was unsure of what to expect next.

"I guess you heard the rumors, Henry, and you really want to tell me that you told me so. Well have at it."

Henry watched the tears well up in her eyes and reached over to take Margaret's hand in his own. She withdrew her hand almost immediately and picked up her glass.

Margaret's mouth was dry. She sipped her iced tea, the ice cubes clattering when she set down the glass. "I'm just so sick of everyone whispering around me as though I can't hear them, I could just scream." She looked at Henry. "I'm sorry the truth seems to be obvious to everyone but me."

Margaret could feel her body heat up from the hormonal changes. For several minutes now, she had seemed to be losing color in her face. "Please, Henry let's not talk about John anymore."

The waitress came over to refill her glass. Setting the pitcher down on the table, she reached up to pull out her pen, which was tucked inside the severe knot of her blonde hair. She stood staring down at her pad as though waiting for Margaret to gain her composure. Margaret and Henry each ordered the cheeseburger and fries.

There was a faint bead of perspiration high on Margaret's forehead. Excusing herself, she got up and went to the ladies' room to pour cold water on her face. She stood for a moment staring in the mirror, dabbing the wetness from her face.

Henry realized that they were becoming more estranged and felt he was taking the backlash for how John had abandoned Margaret. "God, I'm sorry," Henry said when she returned to the table. "I didn't mean to upset you, Margaret." He looked at her for an endless moment, silently wishing he could take back everything he'd said over the previous week. "You all right, Margaret? Your face seems a little pale." He looked at her closely.

Taking another sip of tea, Margaret stared hard at Henry. She knew she could trust him; they had known each other since kindergarten. "I'm pregnant, Henry." She looked down at her food. She was quiet for a moment, picking up a fry and slowly chewing, being careful not to look up to see Henry's expression. "I'm a couple months." She paused, then suddenly picked up her glass of tea and brought it to her lips. Sneaking a peek over the glass's rim, she said, "You're the only one who knows, Henry."

Henry sat quiet, his eyes attentively on Margaret. He thought her face was still pale. Not wanting to further upset her, Henry hesitated before reaching for her hand. He couldn't help thinking that if he was the first to hear those words, he must be the only one she trusted to tell; this made him feel different.

Henry sat up straight. Pulling Margaret's hand towards him, he whispered, "Tell your dad I'm the father."

Margaret couldn't believe she'd heard his words correctly. Her eyes filled with tears as she looked at Henry. "Henry, I'm sorry I told you that. I didn't mean to lay this responsibility in your lap."

There was something in his eyes, something quiet and deep and alive in a way he hadn't been a few minutes before. He was silent for a little while and then glanced at her. "I love you, Margaret."

Margaret wanted to blurt out, "I love you too," but she forced herself to say nothing at all. Those were the words she had longed to hear John say to her again, not Henry. It just all seemed to be going too fast. Henry reached for her hand again, but she quickly drew her hand away, telling him, "It's too soon, Henry."

With a look of desperation, Henry asked, "Too soon for what?" He looked straight into her eyes. "Too soon to tell you I'm in love with you? I want you to be my wife, Margaret! I've been in love with you since kindergarten."

Henry continued to stare at Margaret as she stared down at her food. Henry hoped to regain Margaret's attention, and with further persuasion he said, "I loved you first."

Saying nothing, Margaret pulled herself away from him and got up from her seat and began walking towards the door. Before walking out the door she turned around. The tears were spilling down her face now, and she turned her back to him once again, walking out the door. And yet, deep inside, she still knew Henry was her friend.

Shifting gears, the truck moved towards the lake. Tears streamed down Margaret's face and her heart ached. The cold air could be felt coming from the cracked window as she drove down the path, warmed by her angry words toward Henry. He was the one person since kindergarten with whom she shared most of her fears and dreams; now she had left him sitting at Betty's alone absorbing her cruel words.

Walking into the house a few hours later, Margaret found her dad sitting at the table balancing the farm check book. Looking up at Margaret, he asked, "Did you see Henry?"

Thomas searched her face and saw something strange in her eyes, something hidden and distant. Margaret nodded. "Yes, for a short while at Ms. Betty's. I'm going upstairs to paint." Before Thomas could respond, Margaret already had reached the top of the stairs. Thomas realized Margaret was in trouble - her distant stares and quick exits to the bath-room he recognized from when Jacqueline was pregnant with Margaret. He remembered the morning after the party at the Lodge when Margaret had arrived home in the early morning, how he had sat at the kitchen table reading farm literature when she quietly slipped inside and went straight up to her room. He'd hoped she had been responsible, after all, she was a grown woman who was assiduous about the way she lived her life. After several hours of balancing the farm books, Thomas' tired eyes reminded him of the late night.

Thomas went upstairs quietly and walked to Margaret's room, pacing between the window and bed while she slept.

Thomas remembered the nights following the death of Jacqueline, sitting quietly for hours in the chair beside Margaret's bed, staring at her sleeping and hoping to see any resemblance to her mother. As the years progressed, Margaret had grown into her mother's looks, but had his stubborn ways. Looking down, he saw that Margaret still slept with the two stuffed bears that had both been given to her at her mother's funeral.

Thomas reached down for the white furry one. He wasn't surprised they still occupied the full size bed with Margaret. Margaret's connection to them made it hard for her to put them in the dark closet with the rest of the stuffed animals. Watching her soundly sleep, he reached down to kiss her forehead. Thomas knew he needed to intervene. While Margaret was attending a workshop at a college in Greenville, he would travel up North using the address he'd received from Lawrence at the Lodge to locate John Ashton.

Chapter 15

Thomas arrived in New York City on a cold wet day, tired from the two day trip. As he made his way down bustling 5th Avenue, Thomas realized he had not been here since World War II. He drove slowly, looking for a small hotel where he could take a hot bath and get a good night's sleep before continuing his journey.

Nine-thirty on a Monday was a cold March morning. The brisk air took Thomas's breath away when he stepped outside. Reaching inside his coat pocket, he felt for the folded paper. Unfolding it, he validated the address before handing it to the driver. Staring at the paper, the taxi driver mumbled something in a heavy Italian accent, making it hard for Thomas to understand. Looking in the mirror at Thomas, the driver shook his head.

"Okay," Thomas confirmed.

Suddenly the taxi took off, and Thomas reached for something to hang onto, now even more nervous. The morning traffic was tight. The smell of the city lingered inside the taxi. A dampish-looking cigarette was balanced on the ashtray and every now and then the driver took a drag.

Looking out, Thomas noticed the streets were filled with trash, with almost every corner occupied by homeless people trying to keep warm by huddling over the metal grates, each hoping to capture the warm steam being released by the buildings. Others got their warmth by sipping from brown paper bags. The clear liquid helped to cloud their thoughts from the reality of their existence. All of this was making Thomas homesick for the fresh air and openness of Eastern North Carolina.

As they moved through the city the scenery began to clean up, with streets lined with ornate light posts, and fancy cars parked in front of homes as big as Mattamuskeet Lodge. The taxi stopped, and Thomas heard the taxi driver mumbling something as he handed the paper to Thomas, who looked down at the address and then stared at the address in front of the home.

As Thomas stood frozen not knowing what to do, a voice from the front interrupted his thoughts. "Hey man, this okay?"

Looking down at the paper, Thomas said, "Yeah, okay." Opening the door, he hesitated before stepping out. "You wait, I'll be back."

The dark-haired Italian man held his hand out before Thomas stepped out. "Give me money, I wait." It was obvious he'd been stuck with the taxi fare on more than one occasion.

Thomas reached in his pocket and gave the taxi driver a little more than the fare amount. As he walked up the steps, the massive home caused Thomas to hesitate before proceeding. Looking back, he noticed the driver had laid his head back for a quick nap. The front door was the focal point of the home, with beveled glass inlaid in mahogany wood. A brass bell gleamed at the visitor, who contemplated whether he ought to put gloves on before leaving his fingerprints on the shiny button.

"Damn," Thomas whispered, "What am I doing here?" Each step towards the front door made him feel anxious.

Reaching up, Thomas put his finger on the round brass button. In a few minutes, he could see someone walking towards the door. It was hard to recognize the person, but as he stared at the outline of his features he thought him to be John. Thomas took in a deep breath, not knowing if he could suppress his anger towards the man he had come to know as a good friend during those weeks while he courted Margaret, but who now he realized had only took advantage of his daughter. Thomas had come to despise him.

The young man that flung the door open must have been surprised to see the look on Thomas's face, a look of anger and then disappointment. Regardless, the young man smiled. He had the same smile and facial features as John, but he looked more like a boy a few years younger than John.

Clearing his throat, Thomas hesitated as he tried to get the words out, nervous in this foreign place. "I'm um, I'm sorry, my name is Thomas Windley. I am a hunting friend of Mr. Ashton, um I mean John Ashton. Is he home?"

Before Thomas could finish speaking, the look on the young man's face was of fear, maybe sadness, then the young man spoke about John in the past tense... Thomas put his head down, shaking it back and forth. Thomas apologized for disturbing him, then shook the young man's hand, not exactly sure what to say or do.

All Thomas Windley remembered was that he wanted to get back to North Carolina and home to New Holland, where he belonged. It all made sense now. Thomas told the cab driver to take him back to the hotel. Thomas sat in the back of the taxi, mentally captivated by what he heard. He knew now that this whole thing about John returning back to Margaret would never happen, yet Thomas would never mention anything to Margaret about his trip to New York. When he returned back to the hotel, Thomas packed up what

little he had in the room and drove all the way home without
stopping, his adrenaline not letting him slow down.

When Easter came around, Margaret called her dad, telling him she couldn't make it home for the holiday week
and was thinking about living full-time in Greenville. The
next day, her dad was standing at the door, ready to take her
home. Margaret stood with her face frozen with shock and
tears in her eyes.

Thomas didn't want to make things worse for either
of them; he never mentioned John, not wanting to upset
Margaret. Thomas felt that, all things aside, they needed to
move forward with the present situation. He said nothing
about going to New York. All Thomas wanted was to bring
his daughter home, but it was Margaret who spoke first, as
she put her hands on her belly with a defeated look.

"About four months, I'm sorry dad..." She began to cry,
and Thomas's heart went out to her. He put his arms around
his daughter, and held her close.

"I love you Margaret, don't ever think otherwise. I would
never disown you for being pregnant. I'm behind you all the
way, now and forever. Now, let's get your things packed,
we're going home."

When they arrived home, Margaret walked upstairs
into the white splendor of her own bedroom, feeling hap-
pier than she had in weeks. It was wonderful to be home.
Lying across her bed, she kicked off her shoes and hugged
her stuffed animals. She had hated being away from home,
but felt if her dad knew her condition he would be hurt and
ashamed. Now she knew he loved her more than any creature that walked this earth.

Margaret somehow needed John to know about her preg-
nancy, and so tomorrow she would send word to Lawrence

to get John's address in New York. Rolling on her side, she cupped her belly, feeling his closeness, his warmth. As she pulled her knees forward, lying still in a fetal position, she fell asleep and dreamed. She couldn't stop herself from thinking about him, craving to be happy over something long gone. However, thanks to the creation of a new person to care for, she began to feel good again. The year became the happiest ever.

The baby came home as a small bundle wrapped in the blue blanket knitted by Lillian, who had just known it was going to be a boy. Baby John's birth gave Margaret the will to paint again. Thomas was a big help - he was a natural at being a grandpa, and John was a good baby. He smiled at everyone he met, and everyone doted on him. When the farming season started, Lillian Rogers babysat; she loved being called Grandma. Taking the address Margaret received from Lawrence, she wrote many letters to John about their son, but unfortunately she never received a response from him.

To protect his daughter and grandson, Thomas told Lawrence never to mention anything about John to Margaret. Even when John's friend Nathanial came from New York the following year to hunt, and told Lawrence he had information for Margaret and needed her address, he was told she had left for college, and that Lawrence would forward the information to Thomas. Thomas carried the trip to New York and any information about John to his grave.

Chapter 16

Margaret woke up lying face down on the ground. The loud sound made by the honking goose made her already pounding head hurt worse. Disoriented, she tried to lift herself up, not knowing what had happened. As she looked in the direction of the goose's alarm, she realized she must have fallen, for she only remembered running back to the truck.....and now she was on the cold ground.

It was nearly dark. She closed her eyes for a second. The pain throbbed in the lower part of her right leg. Looking around for something to pull herself up off the ground, she tried to slide forward towards the truck, when she heard a recognizable voice coming from that direction. It was Henry. He had come looking for her.

Margaret yelled in a weak voice, "Here I am!" and Henry came running.

Henry feared the worst when he saw Margaret lying on the ground. When he reached down to gently lift her head, his fears subsided as his eyes met hers. Seeing the tears in Henry's eyes, Margaret realized the enormity of his love for her; a love that never wavered despite all the times she pushed him away. After she wrapped her arm around his neck, Henry lifted Margaret off the ground. Holding her close to him, he asked her where she hurt. The source of her pain was obvious when Margaret's boot hit the tree, making her yell out in pain.

As they reached the truck, Margaret heard two more familiar voices; There stood Claire and John, reaching for her as Henry tried to open the truck door. Claire, who was studying to be a nurse, reached down to examine Margaret's foot. It was severely bruised and probably sprained, but luckily not broken. John nervously helped to put his mom in her truck, and then Henry and Claire loaded up Margaret's things in Henry's truck.

John drove the truck, trying to keep his eyes on Margaret and on the road all at the same time. He was worried about his mom, who still had a headache from hitting her head. Reaching over for her hand, he said, "You going to be okay, Mom?"

Rubbing her head, Margaret really wasn't sure. She still felt groggy, and her upright position didn't help. Putting her hand on her head, she said, "I'm going to be fine, son. My head is still throbbing, but other than my foot aching, I think I'll be okay once I get home and lie down. Thanks for coming out looking for me. I don't remember what happened." Margaret squeezed his hand, and he squeezed back. John smiled, pleased to see that his mom was going to be okay.

Margaret slipped on her flats. Her right foot was still a little sore, but after a week the swelling had gone down. Grabbing the railing, she hesitated before starting downstairs, stopping in front of the full length mirror to adjust her belt.

John grabbed the fire poker to stir the coals in the wood stove. Turning, he smiled at his mother. "Mom, I told you to call me when you were ready to come down! I don't want you hurting yourself."

Margaret smiled, "I love your thoughtfulness son, but I need to manage on my own. You'll be leaving for school in another two weeks." Margaret stepped into the living room to admire the Christmas tree decorated during last night's Christmas party. John had done a fine job picking out the tree.

Stepping into the kitchen, Margaret peered into the large pot where the oatmeal swelled, throwing in a couple sticks of cinnamon to add some flavor to the otherwise bland porridge. Both sat down to eat.

The telephone rang. John grabbed the phone saying, 'Yes sir, she's right here." Before John handed over the phone, he covered the mouthpiece and whispered, "It's Mr. Ashton."

John handed the phone to his mother. Margaret gripped the receiver. Clearing her throat, she said, "Hello." A pause. She listened intently to the voice of the man on the other end. "Yes, Mr. Ashton, I did receive your message. Any time after 2pm will be fine?"

Margaret could feel John's knowing stare. He knew all his mother knew about his father, John Ashton, but neither knew anything about William Ashton. Margaret hung up the phone, then in silence the two finished their breakfast before they left for church.

The White Church stood high in the middle of New Holland. Most families regularly attended the small church, and had since the town had been established. They'd had the same minister for the past five years; he connected well with everyone.

Driving on the gravel, Margaret saw a hand waving at them as they pulled into the parking lot. John waved back and said, "Hey Mom, pull over there beside Claire."

Easing into the parking space, Margaret could see Henry standing outside the church, fumbling for something in his coat pocket. Pulling out his glasses, he paused to read the church bulletin. Margaret gave Claire a hug, thanking her for all she had done to make last night's Christmas party a memorable time. As Margaret slowly walked towards the church door, she realized that Henry stood waiting not to read, but for her to arrive. The two walked together inside the church, both immediately hit by the fresh smell of greenery from the recent Christmas tradition, "The Hanging of the Greens." The church service was a preparation for Christ's coming, which included hanging greenery traditionally associated with everlasting life. Greens such as cedar for royalty, fir and pine boughs for everlasting life, holly symbolizing Jesus' death, and ivy representing the resurrection, festooned every corner and balcony. The tree perched on the alter was generously decorated by homemade ornaments representing the church's family members.

Something about Henry felt different to Margaret. As the two sat in the pew she eased closer beside him. Feeling her warmth, he stretched his arm behind her, laying it across the lip of the pew as if wanting to protect her.

Chapter 17

Sitting on the porch, Margaret could see the car coming up the drive. She nervously stood up as though she wanted to run back inside the house. As the car got closer, she could feel her heart racing. Taking in a deep breath, she quietly stood there alone until Henry came blasting out the door. On the porch, he wrapped his arms around her shoulders. "Margaret, are you okay?"

Taking in another deep breath, she exhaled, "I'll be fine." Before she could say anymore, the slamming of the car doors stopped her words. Standing in the front yard was an older version of John, hesitating as he exited from the vehicle.

Margaret stepped forward to introduce herself. "Welcome, I'm Margaret Windley."

They both stood in the yard for a second, shaking hands as he introduced himself as William Ashton. He waited for the women to exit the vehicle and move to nervously stand by his side. Then, putting his arm around the older woman, he said, "This is my wife, Marianne, and my daughter Sophie."

The two women stood poised, almost copying the others mannerisms. Both, mother and daughter stood 5'6", their petite sculpturesque frames too elegantly over-dressed for the area. Marianne's blond hair was whipped up beautifully and sprayed firmly into place, making her look older than her actual years. Sophie wore her long and thick hair loose around her face. A headband embellished with tiny flowers kept her hair out of her eyes, making her look younger than her 17 years.

Margaret acknowledged them and quickly turned to introduce Henry as her good friend. She blushed when she saw Henry smile and wink at her before extending his hand out to William Ashton. The awkwardness doubled when William asked if there were any other family members. Hesitating for a second, Margaret stared at Henry, then understood who he was asking about. Margaret turned to look up the driveway to see if the farm truck was anywhere in sight. Smiling, she said, "I'm sorry, my son John is out feeding the cows. He should have arrived back by now, but probably stopped to mend the fence. Living on a farm is a constant chore."

Margaret could almost see the relief in William's eyes when she mentioned John's name. Nervously laughing, she apologized for her rudeness. "Why don't we all step inside where it is warm."

Everyone piled inside the living room, and Margaret went into the kitchen. A few minutes later, she returned with a tray of glasses and a pitcher of sweet tea clinking with ice cubes. Seeing her nervousness, Henry took the tray from her hands and set it down on the dining table. Margaret noticed everyone looking at the family pictures, especially the ones of John. She could hear William and Marianne whisper something about resemblance when they picked up John's high school graduation picture.

"That's John's high school picture, taken 3 years ago,"

Margaret cut in. "He'll be graduating from State college next year and recently was accepted to the University of North Carolina's School of Law. He is very excited."

William suddenly remembered he had a box he needed to retrieve from his vehicle, that contained important documents he needed to go over with Margaret. As he walked back with the small box, he asked if there was a dining table they both could sit at to discuss some legal matters. Margaret wasn't sure what he meant, but he assured her he would explain shortly after they sat down.

Henry entertained Marianne and Sophie, showing them photo albums of the Windley family. Margaret could hear Sophie ask about Margaret's paintings, saying her Uncle John had purchased one that was breathtaking many years ago when he came to the Lake Mattamuskeet Lodge. For a while it had hung in his bedroom at her grandpa's house. Before Margaret could turn to ask about the painting Sophie was referring to, William grabbed her hand, telling Margaret that it would all make sense after he went through these documents.

He started to explain, "First, I would like to apologize for inconveniencing you and your family during the holidays, and for what I am about to say. I don't mean to upset you, but recently my father, Howard, passed away, leaving me instructions on dispersing his estate. I am the Executor of his estate. In a letter written by my father to me, left along with his will, he outlines the involvement between you and my brother John."

Margaret could feel her heart beat faster as she stared in disbelief at the seriousness of his words.

Stopping for a moment, William grabbed Margaret's hand. With tears in his eyes, he struggled to get his words out, "I'm sorry to say this, but my brother John passed away many years ago while crossing a street in New York City."

Margaret gasped, she could feel her body trembling with the shock of it. Stunned, she stared at William in disbelief, shaking her head back and forth, quietly whispering to herself, "Everything makes sense now."

Trying to keep it together, her sight blurred from the tears welling up. Quickly she got herself together when the sound of an engine could be heard coming up the path towards the house. Margaret turned to go meet John at the door, but her legs would not move. Before she realized it, the kitchen door slammed. Then John stood in the room, apologizing to everyone for being late; it seemed one of the cows had gotten out.

John went around introducing himself to everyone. When he stood in front of William, William's gasp caught everyone off guard. Tears rolled down his face. Apologizing, he hugged John tightly. "I'm sorry John, I didn't expect the resemblance to be so uncanny. You are like a double of my brother. I'm sorry for the outburst. Please sit, John. I've got so much to tell you."

Grabbing a chair, John assured William there was no need to apologize. Looking around the room, John was taken aback by all the stares.

William again apologized, and asked John to please have a seat.

John hesitated, then Margaret said, "Please, son."

William carefully turned to John, as though he had longed for this reunion for many years. Quietly he asked John, "How much do you know about your father?"

Confused, John stared at his mother. "I know everything my mother knows about him. And I know he left and never returned to her like he had promised, leaving my mother to wonder what happened to him."

William reached over for Margaret's hand. "Do you want me to tell him?" Reluctantly, Margaret shook her head up and down; she was too emotional to say anything.

William Ashton pulled out a stack of legal documents, and explained about the legalities of why he was there. William flipped through several pages, then he came across an envelope tucked between two pages. He pulled it out. Opening it, he explained the letter was from his grandfather, John Howard Ashton, and addressed to his grandson, John.

John opened the letter. Each word was eloquently hand-written by a man who had spent his whole life dictating his words to others. Silently, John read the two- page document. For a second he sat staring at his mother, stunned by all that was taking place. "Mom, Mr. Ashton would like to apologize for all he had put you through, but he knew by reading the letters you sent to dad, I was turning out to be a wonderful grandson."

William turned and said, "Let me explain, Margaret." Turning back to John, he explained, "John, before you walked into the house, I was telling your mom about your father and how he was killed by a careless taxicab driver, not paying attention, ran a red light at an intersection. The taxi struck and killed your father; my brother, as he was crossing the street."

John was saddened by this news even though he had never met his dad. The only memories he had were those told to him by his mother, who had sustained them in her thoughts for many years. Worried about his mother, John got up to sit down next to her and held her hand in his. Margaret looked up at John, and remembered the night she and his father had sat in the exact same spots having dinner for the first time, how that excitement was so different from this.

William asked, "May I continue?" They both shook their heads yes.

William proceeded, saying, "My dad, Howard, was very upset with John when he informed him he would be leaving New York to live in North Carolina, where he planned to marry the most beautiful girl in the world. I can still remember the two shouting back and forth, and how my father had yelled that he would disinherit John if he left. John told him he didn't care about the money, for he had found a woman whom he loved and he would never let her go. He said they would survive living a life of simplicity, and he could practice law anywhere. John slammed the door and left the house for the last time. He had already packed for North Carolina. He was excited but had one last stop to make before leaving: the jewelry store."

Reaching inside his pocket, William handed the neatly wrapped box to Margaret. "My brother was clutching this gift when he was struck by the vehicle. He had just left the store where he purchased an engagement ring for you, Margaret, when he was killed." With sincerity, William again apologized for his father, who had not contacted Margaret after John was killed.

Reaching for Margaret's hand, William took in a deep breath. Looking up to make eye contact with Margaret, he said, "Margaret, my father was a broken man when John was killed. Their last moments together were not good, and the guilt from his angry words to John caused my father a lifetime of grief. Margaret, I know your letters gave him some sense of peace, but unfortunately his pride got the best of him. I am thankful for my nephew, and I am sorry we missed the opportunity to watch him grow-up into the fine young man he is today."

Margaret squeezed his hand, "It's okay William. I truly understand, but I am happy Howard never told me about John's death. Thinking he was still alive gave me hope, the hope he may return back to John and I."

With tears flowing down her face, there was a mixture of emotions as Margaret unwrapped the box. Still inside its satin case was the most magnificent ring she had ever seen. Everyone stood around her and stared in disbelief at the two-caret diamond. Staring at the brilliant cut diamond, she couldn't believe her eyes, and without hesitation she slid the box in John's direction. "I know you love Claire son, please give this to her."

Grabbing her hand, John pulled her towards him, as she cried in his arms. "Mom, Dad loved you very much. I'm glad you now know the truth."

William, noticing Henry standing in the living room, asked him to sit down with John and Margaret; he felt the closeness amongst all of them.

Henry grabbed Margaret's hand as William continued. "My father, Howard, was a defeated man after my brother, John died. He became a workaholic and wanted nothing but to work himself to death. I knew nothing of John fathering a son until I read my father's will. Apparently he opened and read all of your letters to my brother, Margaret, especially the annual letters chronicling everything happening in his grandson's life. I know it must have given my dad a sense of comfort after John's sudden death."

Looking at his mother, John said, "I didn't know you had written all those letters, Mom."

Margaret put her hand on John's shoulder. "I thought your dad needed to know about his son. I never would have guessed he had died. I knew your father was a decent man, but deep down inside I knew something or someone must have kept him from returning to us."

With a look of sadness, William paused before returning to the documents. Taking in a deep breath, he apologized before beginning. "I am sure my father had his reasons for not wanting to contact you, Margaret. The grief apparently took its toll on him. I know he would be proud of his grandson. Unfortunately, my wife Marianne and I are not able to have any more children, but honestly I had to come here in person to witness for myself if John was truly my brother's son. Undoubtedly he is my brother's son, and my nephew. Please don't think ill of me for saying this."

Margaret shook her head no, saying, "Please, I wouldn't."

With sincerity William thanked her, then as though he were addressing the court, the attorney in him stepped forward, quickly articulating his father's wishes. "As stipulated in my father John Howard Ashton's Last Will and Testament: "My son John Howard Ashton Jr's inheritance

125

will be awarded to my grandson, John Ashton Windley, including real estate, stocks and bonds, and my son's interest in the family law firm."

William turned to John. "John, I know you have been accepted to UNC School of Law, but your grandfather would like you to continue the family tradition of attending Harvard. There you will find several buildings named after your father."

John sat speechless, shaking his head back and forth. Finally, he was able to find the words, "I'm a lot like my dad. I think I will enjoy the simplicity of my life for now. Maybe once I adjust to all this, I will see things differently."

Everyone agreed, and smiled at John. William mumbled something about, "In closing." Margaret was relieved all this was about to be over, it was too much already to take in. Henry quietly smiled at her as she stared back at him. She again, found herself thankful he was still by her side, after all she had put him through.

"Oh Margaret, I don't know if you know a Thomas Windley," William began, but before he could get the words off his tongue, Margaret said, "He is my father. Why?"

William interrupted, "He is? I mean, I met your father about three months after John's death. He came to the house looking for John, said he was a hunting buddy of his and he needed to speak with him." Margaret stared at Henry then back at William. "Are you sure it was my dad?"

William nodded. "Looking at the picture of him on the mantle holding John, I recognized him."

Stunned, Margaret turned to Henry. "He went while I was in Greenville."

Putting his arms around Margaret, Henry kissed her forehead and whispered, "Margaret, he only wanted to protect you and John. He knew you had already gone through so much, and once you seemingly got over the heartache, he felt it would be easier not to disturb old feelings, and took it all to his grave."

Holding his mom's hand, John too understood his grandpa's reason for not disclosing the truth.

William Ashton apologized again for his father, Howard. Then the final blow came when he handed Margaret the original deed to the property once owned by Clarence Patterson, adjacent to her property on Lake Mattamuskeet. William took a deep breath and continued, "After John's death, my dad received a call from a Mr. Patterson at the law firm about property John had purchased for his soon to be wife as a wedding gift. They needed to finalize some documents to transfer the deed. My dad said nothing to Mr. Patterson about John's passing and finalized the paperwork himself. For years he never mentioned anything about the property until he noted it in his will. He knew John would have wanted to give you this, Margaret, and he was grateful to you for taking the time to raise a wonderful son and grandson."

Stunned, Margaret couldn't get any words out. Everyone in the room was laughing and crying at the same time. Margaret was so grateful for their generosity and was still speechless.

John promised his Uncle William he would see them during his Easter break, and asked would it be okay if he brought his girlfriend, Claire. Hugging his nephew good-bye, William told him he couldn't wait to meet Claire, and that they would be expecting them at Easter. Margaret and Henry, he said, were also welcome.

As they walked back to the car, Sophie turned to Margaret, telling her how she had always wanted to be an artist like her, and how she would like to study at Parson's in New

York. Margaret smiled. "I always wanted to go there, but things changed, and I'm glad they did."

"Dad brought one of your paintings back," Sophie told Margaret.

Hearing this, William opened the car trunk to pull out the painting. As Margaret unwrapped the package she stood with an unbelieving stare. She couldn't hold back her emotions. She felt a faint wave of nausea, and quickly grabbed Henry. She looked at him for a moment, and then, slowly, a look of excitement at what she saw brought tears streaming down her face.

Margaret pulled back the rest of the paper and just stared. Whispering to herself, she said, "He bought the painting." Her memory visualized John's expression as he tried to distract her from the bidding war. Just as the final bid that sealed the deal was made, John had grabbed Margaret's hand, pulling her away from the room. The only word Margaret had heard coming from the room was when the auctioneer hollered "sold." But how did he do it? He must have gotten someone else to bid for him, possibly Nathanial, his New York friend.

Before they left, William handed Margaret a box of opened letters Margaret had sent to John throughout the years. Margaret grabbed the box, giving it to John to put on the porch. William Ashton apologized one final time for bringing this information during Christmas. Margaret assured William the truth was hard to hear, but hearing it from John's brother had helped to make the severity of it all seem less difficult to comprehend. Everyone agreed; the excitement of discovering each other was the greatest gift any of them could ever receive. They all hugged one another, wishing each other a Merry Christmas, and promising they would all spend Easter together in New York.

As the Ashton's drove away, John reached over and grabbed his mom's hand. Pulling her close, he said, "I love you mom. Thanks for making me who I am today. The fact you never left this area helped me to appreciate the simplicity of our life." The words validated Margaret's years of struggling with the fact she had never gone to New York to search for John. The three hugged.

It was true that every letter had been opened and read by Howard Ashton, yet each one had been neatly folded and put back in the envelope. Thumbing through them all, Margaret noticed one unopened letter, and wondered why he had not opened that one in the very back. Pulling out the aged envelope, she looked at the front and was surprised to see that the letter was addressed to her. The sender was John Howard Ashton, Jr.

Grabbing the envelope, she held it close against her chest. Her heart beat faster. She tried hard to suppress any grief and confusion, her hands trembling slightly as she gripped the envelope. Margaret let out a painful intake of breath, the manifestation caused by years of the unknown. Her body was too numb to feel her emotions, her trembling fingers scanned the front of the envelope, gently rubbing over the letters, visualizing John's hand gripping the pen as he carefully wrote out her name and address.

Emotions flashed across her face, she pulled the letter to her chest, thanking God for sustaining her belief that she would one day find out the truth about John Ashton. Her son, John needed to know about his father. Margaret knew now John Ashton had been sincere about his love for her.

Standing close to her was her son John, made sad by all this. "My God -" He turned to his mom with a look of shock. He gave her a hug, and she could hear his voice trembling. "It's all over, mom – he's dead. I'm sorry we had to wait so long to find out."

Tears sprang to her eyes, and she cried as she hugged him back. Margaret was nineteen years old when she met John Howard Ashton, Jr., now almost twenty years later, the longing to find out answers was over.

Chapter 18

The sound of church bells rang out to remind the small community it was noon. Ding Dong! Ding Dong! Each beat was precisely spaced apart, and the sound seemingly fading when the final burst vibrated through the crisp air. Margaret had a couple hours of chores left before the short winter day ended. Today marked the date she first met John Ashton, and this was the day she had been waiting for to read the unopened letter.

Sitting in her studio, the sun quietly lit up the canvas facing Margaret. This moment seemed long overdue, but now she was finally ready to finish the painting. His eyes – she remembered the gentleness and honesty of John's blue eyes. Taking the paint brush, she made the blank stare come to life. Only in her own soul could she infuse his humble stare onto the canvas. Margaret's eyes clouded over with grief, the tears streamed down her face as she sat staring at his eyes, finally realizing that he was gone. Margaret had never mourned for John; she had never considered him dead. Now she knew that John would never return to Lake Mattamuskeet, back to her.

Breathing hard, Margaret took the pliers from her pocket to bend back the U shaped wire. She pulled back the woven metal panel to step inside the "Do Not Trespass" area beyond the posted sign. Turning around, she used the serrated jaws to reverse the dirty deed.

As she pulled away, Margaret felt something tugging on the knitted yarn of her shawl, making her apprehensive. She quickly looked back - she was snagged by the wire fence. Unlatching herself, she proceeded towards the back of the building.

Reaching her favorite spot, Margaret sat on the steps of the Lodge, staring straight out at Lake Mattamuskeet. Closing her eyes, she inhaled the crisp air, letting it cleanse away all those years she agonized while waiting for John Ashton to return back to her. Margaret reached for the brown bag containing a corked bottle and glass. She sat drinking the red wine and quietly listening to the birds. With her back against the wooden rail, she pulled out the folded paper from her coat pocket, but hesitated before reading. She thought of the one place she and John seemed enthralled to be, the place they had shared some of their last hours together.

Getting up, Margaret walked towards the back of the building. She removed the cardboard from the window pane. Peeking inside, she smelt the dampness inside the neglected room. Reaching up, she unlatched the lock. Grabbing the inside window sill, she pulled herself into the abandoned room where they had spent their last hours dancing together. Margaret could still faintly hear the music playing. As she looked around, her memory lit up images of people dressed in their finest. Their laughter echoed from every corner of the room. A faint shadow of a man left the crowd and ran out of the room holding the hand of a beautiful woman dressed in a green gown.

Holding tight to her flashlight, Margaret followed them, finding her way down the hall and up the stairs. Turning, she aimed the bright disk of light up the spiral staircase towards the natural light at the top of the landing. Pausing for a moment to catch her breath, she flipped the switch off, watching the beacon of light fading back inside the plastic tube.

Looking out, Margaret took in the scenery of water and waterfowl stretching out as far as her eyesight could see. In the distance, the fading sound of a shotgun could be heard echoing through the trees left bare from the cold and wind. Margaret clutched her shawl tighter around her shoulders, the wool stretching, the red shirt underneath peeking through the woven holes. The warmth from the wine helped her tolerate the cold temperatures.

Margaret pulled out the letter written to her by John. Carefully she unfolded it, gently separating the frail accordion folds deeply creased from years of storage. For a second she wavered before reading the words on the personalized stationary. Margaret was blinded by tears as she read the first three words:

"My Dearest Margaret,

Today, I have arrived home after a long day of traveling. Nathanial drove the whole way. He didn't want me to drive; he was worried I was too distracted. The snow began falling harder as we traveled further north. The gloomy drive did nothing to help my uneasiness since leaving you.

My darling, I feel so lost without you. I have treasured every moment with you. I agonized over leaving you so quickly, trying not to torture myself for leaving you during the holidays. The only pleasure I feel is knowing I will return back to you. I will not lose sight of my love for you. Each second without you feels torturous, but a glimmer of ecstasy lingers in me from our last night together.

Dearest Margaret, the love you gave me has permanently stained my heart. I so long to stare into those beautiful green eyes, to kiss those luscious lips again. I can do nothing to relieve my aching heart but hurry back to the very place where I fell deeply in love with you. My love, I will see you on New Year's Eve, but until then I will cling tightly to my memories with you, and like the geese I will migrate back to you.

Love always and forever,
John H. Ashton, Jr."

Clutching the words tightly to her chest, Margaret looked up at the brilliant sunset marbled with oranges, reds, and yellows, making her smile at the momentous sight. As Margaret drove slowly along the country road, the brilliant sunset slowly faded into the countryside. She moved the high collar of her coat more closely around her face and let her thoughts of John evaporate into the landscape.

The wedding took place at the Baptist Church in New Holland. Margaret slowly walked down the aisle in an ivory satin gown. She moved with grace, her head held high, alluring and enchanting. Her stunning bridal hair clip featured sprays of fabulous white feathers found along the edges of the lake. Around her neck she wore a string of pearls that had been worn by her mother at her own wedding, a gift from her father.

At forty-one, her figure was still slim but curvy, and her hair was a darker blond. Her green eyes still sparkled like emeralds of the finest cut. Margaret walked down the aisle on the arm of her son. The matron of honor was Lillian, who stood at the altar with tears streaming down her face, wearing a beautiful mint-colored gown. The church was filled with many of the locals who had sustained her life through the good and bad times; many had waited years for this inevitable moment.

Before handing her to Henry, John gave his mother a hug and kiss on the cheek, and the two tightly embraced. With tears in her eyes, Margaret reached over to squeeze her longtime friend's hand, and Lillian gave her a hug. Turning to face the one person who had never left her side, Margaret beamed at Henry, tears streaming quietly down her cheeks. Henry gently reached over to wipe them away.

Margaret took a deep breath and tried to steady herself, and then suddenly they both were looking at each other. Margaret felt an exhilaration she hadn't felt in years. She was content and finally at peace with life. The preacher solidified their union as husband and wife. Henry looked at Margaret with tears in his eyes, and then carefully he kissed his wife.

As the two stepped out into the crisp cold air, the honking sound of a goose could be heard above. Looking up, Margaret watched the lone bird flying south. Pulling her closer, Henry began to smile at Margaret, pointing up. They both laughed with tears flowing down their faces as they watched another goose flying closer and closer to its mate. The two birds flew side by side as they began their journey.

Henry looked at Margaret, saying, "I've found my mate for life." Then he gently kissed her on the lips.

Sources

Lake Mattamuskeet: New Holland and Hyde County (Images of America: North Carolina) by Dr. Lewis C. Forrest

The Mattamuskeet Foundation, Inc.
http://www.mattamuskeet.org/

The CoastalGuide
http://www.coastalguide.com

Refuge Manager
Mattamuskeet National Wildlife Refuge
Route 1 Box N-2
Swan Quarter, NC 27885

Gibbs Store LLC
35095 U.S. 264
Engelhard, NC 27824
(252) 925-4511
www.gibbsstore.com

Made in the USA
Middletown, DE
20 July 2015